SLEEPER

ERIC WALTERS

SLEEPER

ORCA BOOK PUBLISHERS

Library and Archives Canada Cataloguing in Publication

Walters, Eric, 1957-, author
Sleeper / Eric Walters.
(The seven sequels)

Issued in print and electronic formats.
ISBN 978-1-4598-0543-9 (pbk.).--ISBN 978-1-4598-0544-6 (pdf).--
ISBN 978-1-4598-0545-3 (epub)

I. Title.
PS8595.A598S56 2014 jC813'.54 C2014-901539-9
C2014-901540-2

First published in the United States, 2014
Library of Congress Control Number: 2014935382

Summary: Fast cars and a gorgeous girl await DJ in England, where he tries to unearth the truth about his grandfather's role as a spy—or a traitor.

Orca Book Publishers is dedicated to preserving the environment and has printed this book on Forest Stewardship Council® certified paper.

Orca Book Publishers gratefully acknowledges the support for its publishing programs provided by the following agencies: the Government of Canada through the Canada Book Fund and the Canada Council for the Arts, and the Province of British Columbia through the BC Arts Council and the Book Publishing Tax Credit.

Design by Chantal Gabriell
Cover photography by Paul Brace, Eagle E-Types, Dreamstime, CGTextures and iStock
Author photo by Sofia Kinachtchouk

ORCA BOOK PUBLISHERS
PO Box 5626, Stn. B
Victoria, BC Canada
V8R 6S4

ORCA BOOK PUBLISHERS
PO Box 468
Custer, WA USA
98240-0468

www.orcabook.com
Printed and bound in Canada.

17 16 15 14 • 4 3 2 1

For John, Norah, Richard, Shane, Sigmund and Ted—
it's been such a joy sharing this ride with all of you!

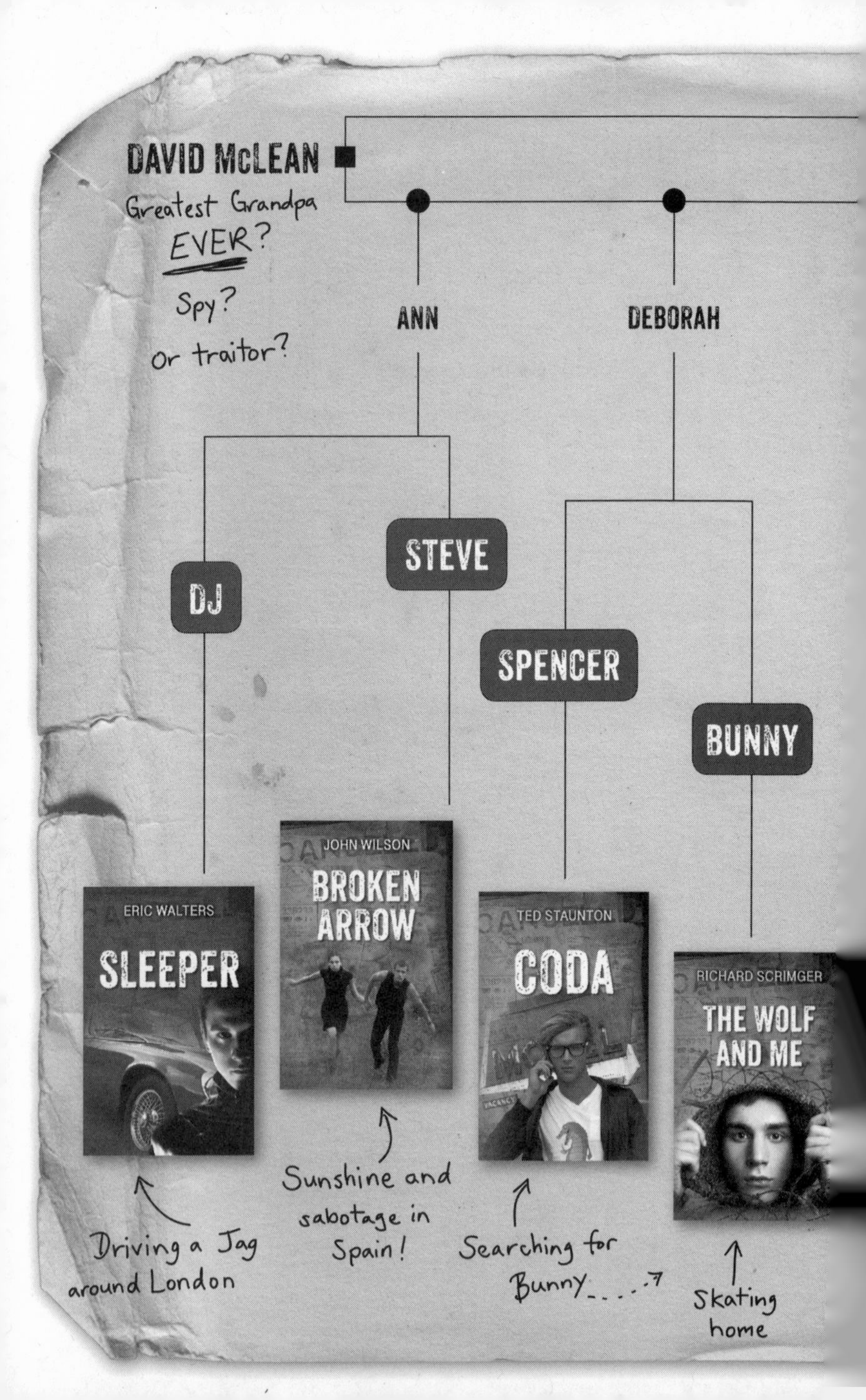
DAVID McLEAN
Greatest Grandpa EVER?
Spy?
Or traitor?
ANN
DEBORAH
DJ
STEVE
SPENCER
BUNNY
ERIC WALTERS
SLEEPER
JOHN WILSON
BROKEN ARROW
TED STAUNTON
CODA
RICHARD SCRIMGER
THE WOLF AND ME
Driving a Jag around London
Sunshine and sabotage in Spain!
Searching for Bunny
Skating home

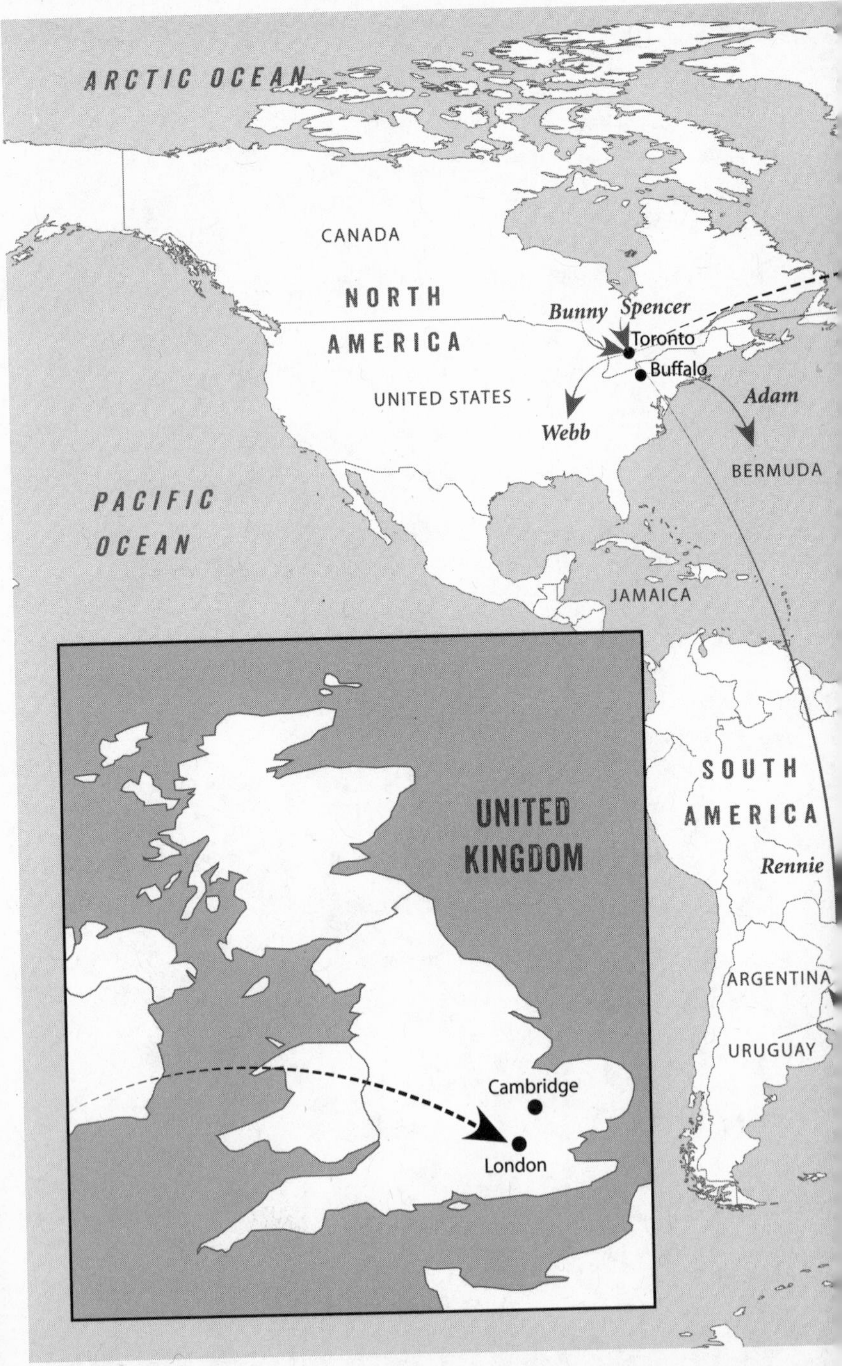

ARCTIC OCEAN

CANADA

NORTH AMERICA

Bunny

Spencer

Toronto

Buffalo

UNITED STATES

Adam

Webb

BERMUDA

PACIFIC OCEAN

JAMAICA

SOUTH AMERICA

Rennie

ARGENTINA

URUGUAY

UNITED KINGDOM

Cambridge

London

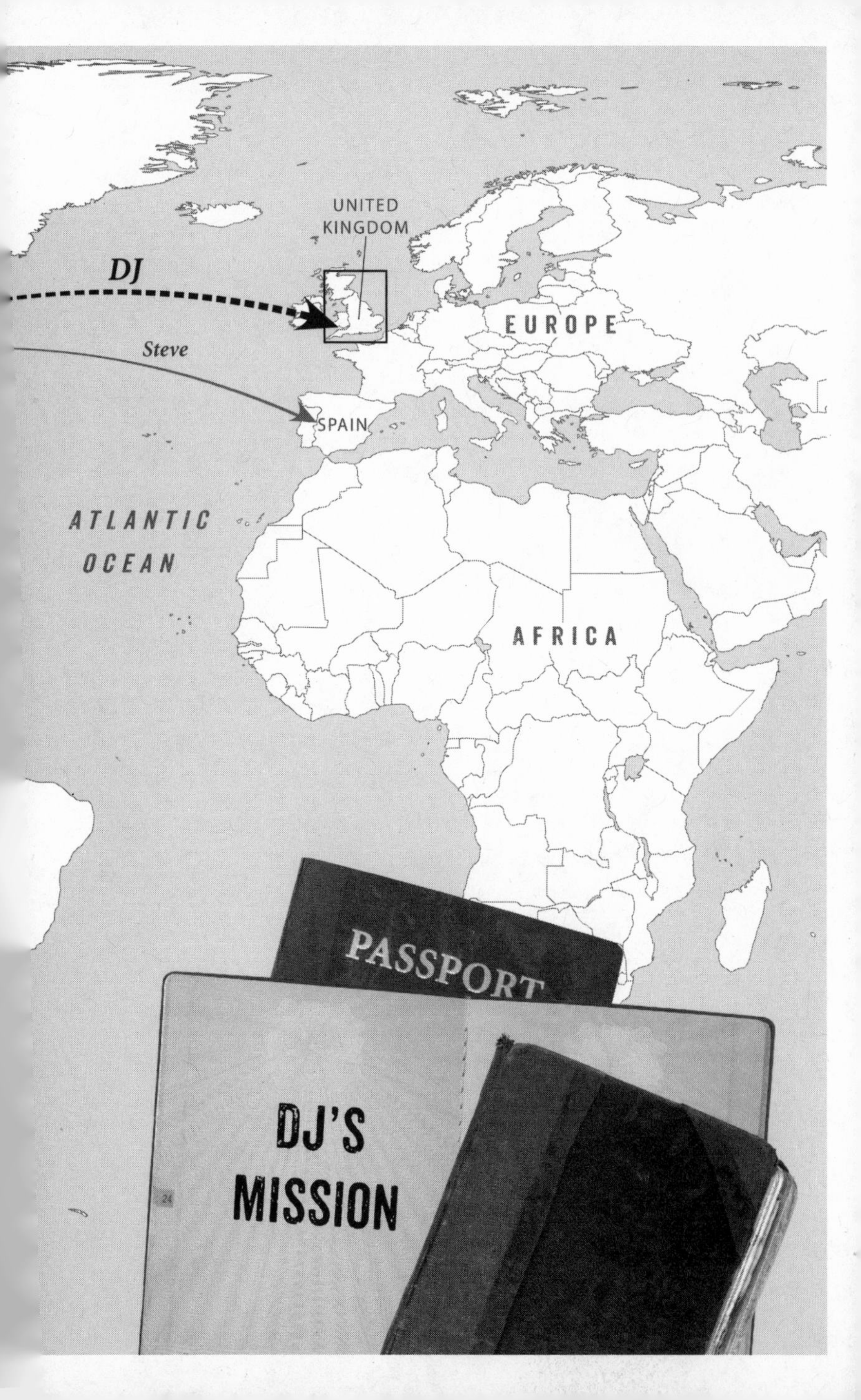

UNITED KINGDOM
DJ
EUROPE
Steve
SPAIN
ATLANTIC OCEAN
AFRICA
PASSPORT
DJ'S MISSION

ONE

DECEMBER 26

There were flashing lights ahead. I pumped the brakes and was relieved when the car responded, slowing down instead of fishtailing on the snow-covered road. I eased over into the empty oncoming lane to go wide around the police car on the side of the road. A police officer was out of his car, helping some people whose vehicle was in the ditch. That was the eighteenth car we'd seen that had gone off the road, along with two transport trucks and a snow-plow. I'd never seen a snowplow skid out, which said a lot about the driving conditions.

I couldn't help but look over at the accident as we went by. The car's occupants, an older couple, seemed to be fine, although there was no way they were getting their car out of the ditch without a tow truck. At least it had been cushioned by the snowbank, which had stopped them from going too far off the road.

"They're okay," I said.

My cousin Spencer looked up from his handheld device. "Who?"

"I said they're okay. They weren't injured."

"Who?"

I almost laughed, but stopped myself. Between the glasses and his response—"who, who"—he did look more than a little like an owl. "There was another car in the ditch," I explained.

He craned his neck to look behind us. "I didn't notice...sorry."

"Don't be sorry. Keep working."

"Okay, thanks." He turned back to his tablet.

Spencer was sitting in the passenger seat beside me, but he had been somewhere else most of the trip. He was in first-year film school and was doing some editing on a project for one of his classes.

He'd occasionally mutter something, but for the most part he was totally absorbed in what he was doing. He had said he wanted us all to see it when it was done. I got the feeling that if we did go off the road and were upside down in the ditch, hanging from our seat belts, he would hardly notice. And when he did notice, he would want to make a movie about it. Grandpa had always said, *Follow your passions.* He would have been proud of Spencer.

Grandpa had been on my mind a lot the last few days. Not that he was ever that far away from my thoughts, but going to his cottage brought back so many memories. He had been gone for over six months, but somehow I expected that when we got there, he'd be waiting on the porch, the cottage warm, a big fire going, the snow shoveled, hot chocolate waiting and stories to share.

"Are we almost there?"

I startled a bit at the voice coming from right behind me. Spencer's younger brother, Bunny, had been asleep so long I'd forgotten he was there.

"Yup, it's the next turnoff."

"Good."

"It's been a long drive," I said.

"It's beautiful up here. All the snow and the *openness*."

"It is beautiful, for sure."

"And open. I like open. There is no open in jail."

Bunny—Bernard was his real name—had just been temporarily released from juvie. He was one of the last people I would have expected to end up in jail to begin with, and definitely *the* last person I expected to survive it. I guess I'd seen too many movies about prison. But the way he described it made it sound more like extended summer camp than jail. That didn't mean it was that way—that was just how he saw it.

My cousins Spencer and Bunny were a little... different. The three of us and my brother Steve had all gone to the same high school, and more than once I'd had to step in when somebody was picking on Bunny or ragging on Spencer. Spencer saw the world from a unique perspective, but Bunny was simply odd. Nice but odd. *Very* odd. There was no other way to describe him. He hardly ever seemed to have much more than a vague understanding of what was happening around him. I guess that might be an advantage in juvie. And now, even if he had been awake for the entire drive, the conditions wouldn't have worried him. Worrying was more my job.

The turnoff appeared just ahead, and I slowed us down to practically nothing and made the turn. The tires grabbed the gravel underneath the crust of beaten-down snow. The road had been plowed, but there was still a dusting of freshly fallen snow on top. We'd have clear sailing through the last section.

"I'm glad we came up here," Bunny said.

"So am I. Grandpa would have liked it."

We were coming up to spend a week at the place Grandpa had loved the most. Five of the six of us... no, five of the *seven* grandsons were coming up. I felt bad about not including Rennie in the original count, but it had only been since Grandpa's death that we had even known we had another cousin. Rennie wasn't going to be with us at the cottage, since he was on vacation in South America with his father, and my brother Steve wasn't here either. His choice. I glanced at my watch. From Steve's text I knew he was already on the train, headed for Seville. He had touched down in Spain two days ago and had been given an enthusiastic greeting from Laia, the girl he'd met in the summer. So there he was, with no snow, lots of sun and a beautiful girl. He'd bugged out on our get-together, but I did understand it. Honoring Grandpa was one thing. Hot girl trumped that every time. Still, I was a bit annoyed and maybe a little jealous.

Our other two cousins, Adam and Webb, were driving up from the States together and might even be at the cottage when we arrived. Part of me wanted them to get there before us—get a fire started to warm the place up—but a bigger part wanted to arrive first. It was hard to put aside my competitive-ness, even for things that didn't matter in the least. Steve always joked that I could turn washing dishes into a sporting event. He was right. I could make anything into a competitive sport and win.

Adam and Webb had really connected over the past months. Spencer had Bunny, and of course Steve and I had each other the way only twins could, and now Adam and Webb had each other. Webb had even stayed with Adam and his parents over the summer. That left only Rennie out of the mix, although Adam seemed to be trying to draw him in; the two of them were Facebook and texting buddies. That was great. It would be hard to be the one on the outside. Rennie had invited all of us to come visit him, and Steve and I were going to take him up on that. Next summer Steve and I were going to go to England for two weeks to visit my friend Doris and then spend two weeks with Laia in Spain. Laia was going to spend some time in Canada before that so I'd get to know her. I couldn't help but wonder if she was as wonderful as Steve thought she was. The most significant difference between Doris and Laia was that Doris was in her late sixties. She had promised to introduce us to a couple of her granddaughters and have them show us around London.

While we were at the cottage, our mothers were also spending time together. The "girls" were going away on a cruise, something they had often done with Grandpa when they really were girls. It was one of the bequests in his will—just like the requests made of his seven grandsons. It would have been simpler if he'd paid for the seven of us to go on a cruise instead of on far-flung adventures around the world, but simpler wasn't necessarily better.

Hardly a day went by that I didn't think about my experience climbing Kilimanjaro, and never a day went by when I didn't think of Grandpa. His beret—the one he always wore, the one he'd given me, the one I'd taken to the top of the mountain—sat atop my head. I still felt like it didn't look right on me, but my mother thought one day it would really "fit."

We came over the last rise in the road and there was the driveway. *David McLean* was written in large ornate letters on the side of a mailbox that marked the way. It was a wonderful old handmade mailbox. Grandpa had made it to look like a beehive. He had been as mad as a hornet himself when the snowplow smashed into the pole and knocked it over a few years ago. Thinking about snowplows made me realize that the driveway was plowed the way it always was. I hadn't been expecting that. It was great, since it meant we didn't have to park on the road and walk down the lane, but it was still a little eerie. It was sort of like Grandpa had done it in expectation of our arrival. It must have been our mothers though. They inherited the cottage, and I was sure they'd contracted somebody local to blow out the driveway.

I eased the car up the lane. I didn't want to end up in the ditch this close to the end of our trip. I noticed that there were no other tire tracks in the inch or so of new snow. We were the first to arrive.

Yeah, we won...and now our prize was to make the fire before the others got here. Maybe second place sometimes was better.

The tires spun as we hit the incline. I geared down and then gave the car more gas, which caused more spinning, but we had enough traction to get to the top of the hill, and there it was—the cottage. The sight made me smile. What had started as a simple building—a couple of bedrooms and a small living area wrapped around a stone fireplace—had grown and grown and grown. Grandpa called it his continual construction project as he added new rooms to provide places for each of us to call our own. He loved building and tools and puttering, and the cottage allowed him to do all those things.

All of this was so familiar, but today there were two things that made it different. There was no smoke rising from the chimney, and no Grandpa waiting at the door. I felt happy and sad at the same time. Happy to be here, sad that he wasn't. I pulled up and stopped, turning off the engine.

Spencer looked up from his tablet. "Oh, we're here...I'm not quite finished."

"Do you want me to drive around a bit until you're done?" I asked.

"No, it's okay. I can finish it...oh, you're joking." He smiled.

"I am. Come on."

We all grabbed our bags and climbed out. While the driveway had been plowed, the path to the porch and the porch itself were still covered in snow over a meter deep. Bunny started bouncing through the snow, not so much breaking a path as imitating, well, a bunny. He giggled and flashed us a silly grin that made me smile back.

"It's locked!" he called out.

"Keys," I said, holding them up. "Catch!" I tossed them and Bunny snatched them out of the air, making a perfect grab. That didn't surprise me in the least. Bunny was a strange combination of coordinated and klutzy. He could catch a football like his hands were made of flypaper but could trip over his feet running a route. And then there was a fifty-fifty chance he'd run in the wrong direction after he caught the ball.

"It's stuck!" Bunny yelled out.

"Give it a shove."

The door gave way suddenly, and Bunny and his bag tumbled into the cottage. I got there in time to see him pick himself up off the floor.

"I got in," he said.

"Now all we need is light and heat."

It was still light enough outside to see, but inside it was dim bordering on dark. I pulled out my cell phone and used it to light a path across the living room and into the kitchen. My Grandpa's golf bag leaned against the wall as if waiting for him to come back. I remembered a joke he always told about God and him playing golf together some day. Strange, I'd heard him tell the joke a hundred times, but I'd completely forgotten the punch line.

I flipped open the breaker box cover and hit the breaker switch, and the ceiling light came on as well as the light in the living room. One out of two things was done; now we needed heat.

"There's hardly any firewood," Spencer said.

Where there was usually wood piled high on both sides of the fireplace, there were only a few pieces. Of course, that made sense. Without Grandpa, there was nobody to cut the wood. That wouldn't be a big problem. An ax was in its usual place, leaning against the wall behind the front door, and there'd be wood piled under the deck.

Bunny reached over and picked up the ax. "In jail they don't let you have anything sharper than a butter knife, so this is real cool. I can get some wood. I like chopping."

He was the most likely candidate to chop off his own foot, but who was I to point that out? "Go for it. We'll use the few pieces that are left to get the fire started."

"I can help with the fire," Spencer offered.

I began scrunching up pieces of old newspaper and tossing them into the fireplace; then Spencer started to pile in some kindling and the few remaining pieces of wood. Bunny opened the door, and I heard the sound of a car.

"Adam and Webb are here!" Bunny called out.

Bunny had left the front door open, and cold air and snow flowed in. As I went over to close it, there was a loud thump behind me. I turned around and saw that part of the wall—a panel, really—beside the fireplace had fallen open. Spencer stood up. In one of his hands was a piece of firewood. In the other was a pistol!

TWO

Spread out in front of us on the table was everything that had spilled out when the wall panel had fallen open. Normally, it would have been hidden and held in place by the stack of firewood.

"I pulled the last piece of wood and it didn't want to come, so I *really* pulled it and the panel fell open," Spencer explained.

"You really must have given it a yank," I said. "That last piece was nailed down and you pulled out the nails."

"I guess I'm stronger than I look."

"That's a lot of money," Webb said, looking at the table.

We had sorted the money by currency and then stacked it in piles.

"It's pretty. It looks like Monopoly money," Bunny added.

"The American money is real," Adam said.

"What are the final counts?" I asked.

"Ten thousand dollars American and ten thousand Canadian," Adam said.

"And exactly five thousand British pounds and another five thousand Euros," Webb added.

"I counted two hundred thousand Argentinian pesos. I'm not sure how much that's worth, whether it's a little or a lot," I said. "Spencer?"

"Oh, yeah, there are one hundred and twenty thousand Russian rubles."

"This makes no sense," I said.

"Maybe Grandpa didn't trust banks," Adam said. "I've heard about old people who stuff money into their mattresses and under their beds."

"Should we check the mattresses?" Bunny asked.

"I don't think that's necessary," I said, although now that he'd mentioned it, I wondered if we should.

"The money I understand, sort of, but why is there a mesh bag full of golf balls?" Adam asked.

"You know how much Grandpa loved golf," Bunny said.

Everybody knew he was a golfer. A few times a year, he'd gone on golf trips down south. "That still doesn't explain why the golf balls were behind the panel. Why hide them?" I said.

"They must have been his favorites," Spencer said. He picked one up. "Funny markings."

"Those are letters—Russian letters," Adam said.

"The golf balls are weird, but the pistol doesn't make sense at all," I said. "He *hated* guns and thought only police and the military should have them."

"Remember how he used to say that *the only weapon a man should have in his hands is a golf club*?" Adam said.

"*Because then the potential wounds are self-inflicted*," three of us said in unison, and we all laughed. That was another one of Grandpa's regular jokes.

"If I had that much money in my cottage I'd want to have a gun around too," Adam said.

"It's not *just* a gun," Spencer said. "This is a Walther PPK."

"Since when do you know about guns?" I asked.

"I don't know about guns, but I know about the gun James Bond used in all the movies."

"James Bond?" Adam said.

Webb laughed. "The reason we were late is we just saw the latest James Bond movie."

"It's the third time I've seen it," Adam added.

"And you recognize the gun?" I asked.

"Well, not really," Adam said.

"But I do," Spencer said. "The documentary I'm working on for my school assignment is about agents, spies, moles and double agents."

"Does that mean Grandpa was a secret agent?" Bunny asked.

"Of course he wasn't," I said. "He was in the import/export business."

"Which would be a good cover for being a spy," Adam added.

"It would explain the things in the bag. Maybe it's an emergency escape bag."

Along with the money, gun and golf balls was a small black leather bag, and inside it, now strewn across the table, was a change of clothing, dark sunglasses, a big floppy hat and a fake beard and mustache.

"That's the sort of thing a spy would use," Spencer explained. "That and the money would allow him to escape at a minute's notice."

I picked up the bag from the table, turned it over and then looked inside to make sure it was empty. I ran my hands along the bottom, inside and out. It was smooth and clean...and too thick.

"Can somebody get me a knife?" I asked.

"You could have a gun if you want," Bunny said. He went to pick it up, but, thankfully, Spencer stopped him.

"I've got a knife," Webb said. He reached into his pocket and pulled out a jackknife, opening the blade. He gave it to me handle-end first.

I wanted to ask him why he had a knife, but I didn't. I turned the bag over, hesitating for just a second, and then plunged the tip into the bottom. The soft leather sliced easily, opening up the body to reveal some stuffing, a few pieces of stiff cardboard... and a passport. I pulled it out, then found a second, third and fourth. I dumped the bag upside down once more and at least another half-dozen passports spilled onto the table. We scrambled to pick them up and look at them.

"This is British," I said.

"And this one is from Spain," Webb said.

"This one's American," Adam added. "Just like mine."

"I've forgotten how to read!" Bunny said. "This one is just a bunch of squiggles to me!"

Webb took it from him and looked at it. "It's Russian. They use a different alphabet."

Bunny looked relieved.

"But why would Grandpa have a bunch of passports?" I asked.

"A better question is, why would Grandpa have passports from different countries in different names but with his picture?" Spencer said.

He opened the British passport he was holding. Inside was a picture of Grandpa—taken when he was young—with the name *Nigel Finch* underneath.

"He's in this one too," Webb said. "But this time his name is Pedro Martinez."

"German," Spencer said. "In this one, he's a German citizen named Helmut Schmid."

"Grandpa spoke German," I said. "And some French and Spanish. He said he needed those languages to import from those countries."

"Or because spies need to speak different languages," Spencer said.

"He wasn't a spy," I said.

"Then what other explanation do you have?" Spencer asked.

"Well...I don't know."

"Maybe the answer is in here," Adam said. He was standing by the fireplace, holding up a small black notebook. "It was tucked into the back corner, almost invisible."

"Can I have it...please?" I asked.

Adam hesitated but then handed it to me.

My head was spinning. I had to slow things down to make sense of it. I opened it to the first page. There was a note in my grandfather's handwriting.

"*I hoped I'd never have to use this book,*" I read out loud, "*but I needed to keep my own record, my own account, in case things ever came tumbling down around me. Maybe I know better than anybody that you can never trust anything or anyone, and I needed proof of who I was and what I did. I just know that I always did what needed to be done. Nothing more and nothing less.*"

"What does that mean?" Bunny asked.

"I'm not sure. Just let me think." I started flipping through the pages. "It looks like it's divided into sections, and each one starts with a date in the far right corner." I did some rough calculations in my head as I flipped back through the pages, looking at the numbers. "The dates go in sequence and are all from times when Grandpa was in his thirties, forties and fifties." I went back through the sections. "There are twelve sections."

"What else is there?" Webb asked.

"Nothing that makes sense to me. There are random series of numbers, diagrams, illustrations and sentences, but the words don't make sense."

"That could be code," Spencer said. "Secret code."

I turned the pages, and an envelope dropped out of the book; Adam scooped it up and studied it intently.

"There's something here," he said. "Not words, but the imprint of words."

He turned it around so that we all could see. "It looks like somebody wrote something and he pressed so hard on the paper that the words are imprinted right here on the envelope. *You are a traitor* and *You deserve to die.*"

"Still think he wasn't a spy?" Spencer asked.

"Maybe he was a spy, but he wasn't a traitor," I said.

Everybody started to talk all at once, and then there was an explosion and we all jumped. Bunny sat there, holding the gun, smoke coming out of the barrel! He had fired it! There was a hole in the wall right above our heads.

"I didn't know it was loaded," he apologized.

"Give me the gun," Spencer commanded.

Bunny turned toward Spencer, and the gun turned with him. Spencer ducked and Adam grabbed the pistol and took it from Bunny.

"It was very loud," Bunny said. "I've never fired a gun before."

"And hopefully never will again," Adam said.

"But none of this is helping us," Webb said. "What do we do now?"

"Maybe we should call our moms," Bunny suggested.

"And tell them what? That their father was a spy or a traitor or something worse?" Webb asked.

They started to argue.

"Could everybody just be quiet?" I yelled. They stopped talking. "Just let me think this through, please!

There has to be something else. He said there was proof in here. We just have to find it."

I started to flip through the pages again. There had to be something here; I just had to see it. Then I saw the little diagram in the bottom corner of a page. It was a crudely drawn UK flag. I flipped to the next section, and in the same place on the page was a flag that I recognized from the World Cup as being from Argentina.

"How many passports are there?" I asked.

Spencer counted them. "Twelve."

"Maybe I do understand," I said. I ripped out the first three pages of the book—the first section—and everybody gasped.

"What are you doing?" Adam yelled.

"Put these with the passport from England." I ripped out the next three pages. "And put these with the Argentinian passport."

There were twelve sections, twelve little maps of the world and twelve matching passports.

"Okay, they connect," Webb said. "What now?"

"Probably nothing," Adam said. "Well, short of going to the places in the notebook and trying to figure it out."

Everybody stopped talking, and I knew we all had the same thought. Who was going to be the first to voice it?

"We can figure it out. We have almost a week before our parents will even know we weren't here," Spencer said.

"And enough money to get wherever we need to go," Adam added.

I picked up the Spanish passport and the notes that went with it. "Steve is already in Spain." I wished he was right here to help make sense of things. As soon as I had a minute, I'd text him and try to explain what had happened—assuming I could explain it to myself.

Webb nodded his head, and a grin came to his face. "We could do it, right?"

Everybody turned to me. "I think it's even more than we *could* do it," I said. "We *need* to do it. One more adventure that Grandpa didn't even know he was going to send us on!"

THREE

DECEMBER 27

"Come on, come on, hurry up," I muttered, as if my words would make the scanner work faster.

My flight was leaving in less than thirty minutes, at 8:10 PM, and I had to email Steve the pages of the notebook. He had to actually see the pages because there was no way I could describe, translate or explain them—any more than I could interpret the pages that were powering me forward.

The last scan went into my computer. We'd already exchanged texts, and I'd tried to explain the craziness to him, but it was all so hard to put into words. I even added a few pictures that I'd taken with my phone, hoping that each picture was worth a thousand words.

Hey Steve,

Attached are some pictures from the cabin that I snapped, the pages from Grandpa's notebook that apply to Spain. I don't know what they mean any more than I know what my pages about England mean but you've always been good with puzzles. If you can figure any of it out let me know and I'll do the same. I've also scanned relevant pages from his fake Spanish passport. I don't know if there's enough here to help you but at least you're already in the right country.

My plane leaves almost immediately and I'll be in England by early tomorrow morning. I've contacted Doris and she's going to help me—although I have no idea what she's going to help me with. None of this makes sense. This might be nothing more than a strange vacation. At least you and I will be in the same time zone.

Finally, I've transferred 2000 Euros into your PayPal account. I don't know if the money will help but I thought it wouldn't hurt to have it.

DJ

I pushed *Send* and it was gone. Now it was time for me to go.

DECEMBER 28

The wheels touched down and I opened my eyes, finishing up my silent prayer for a safe landing. I hate flying. I hadn't slept all night during the flight, and now it was morning in England. It wasn't just the adrenaline rush produced by my fear of flying that had kept me awake: I had been concentrating, trying to figure out what the notebook pages meant. So far all I had done was make myself a little crazy and almost cross-eyed. Eight hours of flight, and it was all still a mystery. I was no further ahead, just thousands of kilometers farther away from home on a fool's mission with almost no clues.

The longer I looked at it, the less it seemed to make sense. I guess being up almost forty-eight hours wasn't helping my ability to focus or think. I needed to get some sleep.

As we taxied to the gate, I did a mental inventory. In my pocket was my passport, my cell phone and my wallet. In the wallet was two hundred pounds. The rest of the five thousand pounds—minus airfare—was in the bottom of my carry-on luggage, right beside Grandpa's fake passports from England and Spain. I pulled out Grandpa's beret—*my* beret—and put it on my head, adjusting it. It still didn't feel completely right, but it was getting to feel more like it was mine.

The plane came to a stop, the seat-belt light went out, and I carefully folded and tucked the notebook pages beside my wallet and then joined everybody else in jumping to my feet. I knew it made no sense. We weren't going anywhere until the doors opened, and even then there'd be a wait for luggage before getting to customs. I wouldn't have to wait for bags though, because everything was in my carry-on. I could go straight to customs and, if I hurried, I could get there first. I really didn't want to keep Doris waiting for me in the terminal any longer than I had to. She had been incredibly surprised when I'd called the day before to tell her I was coming, but she still sounded happy to have me come. Not surprising, since she was such a kind and gracious person. We were nearly fifty years apart in age, but she was still my friend.

The doors opened, and the first-class passengers started to get off. I could have bought a first-class ticket—I had the money—but I just couldn't bring myself to do it. In the end we'd have to tell our parents what we had done, and I'd have enough to explain without having to justify the extravagance of a first-class ticket. I grabbed my bag from the overhead compartment and shuffled down the aisle, nodding goodbye to the steward as I left the plane.

People moved slowly down the corridor ahead of me. I sidled by a few but was stopped by a roadblock of slow-moving passengers. When we reached the actual terminal, the crowd opened up enough for me to get by the first bunch of people. The terminal was loud and crowded, and a line of passengers from the plane stretched out in front of me. I was now in an unacknowledged, unofficial race. I was going to get through before anybody else, including the first-class passengers. I knew that the first people off the plane had a big head start, but I was fast and I had the advantage of being the only one aware that a race was on.

I doubled my pace, moving around people. This was one crowded terminal. I guessed it had a lot to do with the holidays. I had gotten one of the last available seats on both my flight here and the return flight on January 3rd. It seemed like a long way to come for such a short time, but I didn't have any longer. As it was, I was going to be back at the Toronto airport only a few hours before my mother's flight was due in. I'd be there to pick her up.

"Sorry," I said as I bumped into a man who had stopped to tie his shoelace.

People from many other flights were all heading to customs. It was time to open up the competition to not just people from my flight, but passengers from *all* flights. I started to jog. It felt good to move after being cooped up on the plane. I was practically running as I passed by the baggage carousels and the waiting crowds. Up ahead I saw a big sign: *PASSPORT CONTROL.*

I felt a surge of energy as I pushed through the double doors. There were a dozen lines, and none of them had more than one or two people. One of the wickets opened up as a family moved through; I raced over and skidded to a stop before a couple behind me could get there.

"You seem in quite the hurry, lad!" the customs agent said.

"I am. I practically ran from the plane."

"What's her name?" he asked.

"What?"

"What's her name, the young lady meeting you on the other side?"

"Her name is Doris," I said, although I didn't mention she wasn't so young.

"Doris! That's me mother's name! Nice to know it's coming around again!"

I pulled out my passport and handed it to him.

"Do you have anything to declare?" he asked.

"Nothing at all."

"No food products, alcohol or tobacco?"

"I don't smoke or drink and I don't have any food with me."

"And you just have that carry-on bag?" he asked.

"That's all."

He looked at me suspiciously, and I had a flashback to the last time I went through customs, in Tanzania, on my way to climb Kilimanjaro. That time I had been detained, searched and thrown in jail on suspicion of drug trafficking before they realized it was just my grandpa's ashes hidden in the cane I carried.

"If I hadn't seen you running, I would be more suspicious of you sweating so much...but you do look awfully nervous," he said.

I had to think fast. It wasn't like I could tell him about the incident in Tanzania. "I am really nervous, I guess. I haven't seen Doris for six months, and I guess I wonder if...if...you know...if she still cares for me."

He smiled sympathetically. "It's been a while since I was young, but to be honest with you, my missus, Anita, still makes me feel the same way after twenty-eight years of marriage."

I smiled back. This was going to work. He scanned my passport, and his whole expression changed. He turned away and motioned somebody over. Almost instantly two police officers, both wearing sidearms, appeared.

"Take this man away for a secondary inspection, please," he said to the officers.

"But I thought that—"

The two officers led me away. I knew there was no point in fighting or arguing. It had to be some sort of mistake, and it wasn't like I was smuggling drugs or even a forbidden food product. It would all be quickly sorted out. I had nothing to worry about. So why was my heart pounding so wildly?

It wasn't a jail cell, but it certainly was a detention room. I sat on a little metal chair. The only other furniture in the room was a second chair in the corner and a metal table at my side. It reminded me of the tables they have in doctors' examination rooms. One of the police officers remained on guard next to the thick door I had come in by. He stood there, arms folded across his chest, staring at me. I had tried to start a conversation a couple of times, but he was having none of it.

The walls of the room were gray concrete, unmarked and without a single picture hanging up. It actually was like a jail cell. I wondered how thick these walls were...could somebody outside hear me scream? Okay, that was just paranoid, although that officer certainly looked menacing and nobody knew I was here. I wanted to ask if somebody could at least let Doris know what was happening, but I figured there was no point in even trying to ask my guard.

I'd been in here close to an hour already and I knew she'd be worried.

The door opened and two men walked in. They wore almost identical suits and ties and similar shiny dress shoes. They looked alike, too, as if they were more than brothers but slightly less than twins. The major difference was that one of them was carrying my bag. He said something to the police officer, who turned and left, closing the door behind him. They came toward me until they were standing over me. They pushed in close, threateningly, and I felt scared.

"You are David Adam McLean?" one of them asked.

"Yes...yes, sir."

He pulled out my passport and opened it. He held it out and seemed to be comparing me to my passport picture.

"Did you really think you could just sneak into the country without being detected?" the second man asked.

I shook my head. "I wasn't sneaking anywhere. I was coming to visit and—"

The first man cut me off. "And your passport lit up our system like a Christmas tree."

"I don't know what you mean." I really didn't have the foggiest idea.

"I suggest you stop playing dumb," he said.

I wasn't *playing* anything.

"We can do this one of two ways," he said. "The hard way or the easy way. Which is it going to be?"

"I like the easy way."

"Fine. Then tell us what we need to know. Tell us why you have attempted to enter our country."

"I'm visiting a friend. I met her while climbing Kilimanjaro last year, and she invited me to come to England someday."

"Isn't it unusual to purchase a plane ticket with cash?"

I wondered how he knew I did that, but thought I shouldn't ask. "I had the cash and I don't have a credit card."

"And your only luggage is your carry-on."

"It's all I need," I said. "I'm only staying a few days."

"Only a few days and that decision must have been very sudden since you purchased the ticket yesterday. Do you always make such sudden decisions?"

I couldn't tell him the truth. "I had a chance to come over and I had an invitation, so I jumped at the chance. You know love." It had worked with the customs agent—maybe it would work now.

He smirked. "So you are in love with a sixty-seven-year-old woman named Doris?"

How did he know her name was Doris? "Um... yes...you know the way I love my mother and grandmother and—"

He slammed his fist on the metal table, and I jumped. "Do you take us for fools?" he demanded. "I guess it will have to be the hard way."

"Suits me," the second man said. "I *enjoy* the hard way." He smiled. He was slightly larger and more menacing than the other guy. He looked like he would enjoy it.

"We'll start by searching your bag," he said.

"Search away; there's nothing in there but my clothes and a toothbrush."

"And if we don't find anything in there, you'll be searched," he said. "Outside—and then inside, by the medical team."

"Inside?" I gasped.

"Every little crevice and crack. Then you'll be x-rayed and held to see if you have swallowed something that will pass in time."

"You just sit there, buck naked, in a glass room with a glass toilet. Eventually, everything passes. We're in no rush," the second man said.

"This is all a terrible mistake!" I exclaimed. "You have the wrong person."

"We have the right person, David Adam McLean of Canada. There is no question. Let's start with the bag."

He unzipped the bag. Thank goodness all he was going to find was my clothes...until he got to the bottom. That's where he'd find over four thousand pounds in British currency and my grandfather's fake passports—two different countries and two different names with the same picture. The money would be hard to explain, but the passports would be impossible. There was no way out of this, no way to escape what the "hard part" was going to lead to.

The door opened and another man, much older than the other two, entered the room. Any thought of him being here to rescue me vanished when I looked at his expression. He was scowling, and when he looked at me that scowl seemed to deepen.

"Can I help you?" one of my captors asked him.

"I rather doubt it," he said. He opened up his jacket to reveal a badge.

"Oh, sorry, sir. We didn't know contact had been initiated with your level of the section," the larger one sputtered. Suddenly he didn't look as much menacing as apprehensive.

"My level was instantly contacted. Even someone as junior as yourself should know that."

"Would you like us to leave, sir?" the other asked.

Whatever his section or level or rank was, he certainly was above these two, and they knew it and acted accordingly.

"Before you leave, I need to ask a few questions. Is this David Adam McLean?"

"Yes, sir, it is."

He looked at me and then back at them. If looks could kill, they both would have dropped dead before my eyes.

"If I were to suggest that this young man was twenty-eight years old, would you find that hard to believe?" the man asked.

"I believe his passport states that he is—"

"I did not ask you to look at the passport!" he snapped. "I asked a simple question. If I told you this person was twenty-eight years old, would you believe me?"

"I would believe whatever it was that you told me to believe, sir," the larger of the two answered defensively. Now he definitely looked nervous.

"As would I," the other added.

"How about if I were to say that he was actually thirty-eight?"

Both men looked increasingly uneasy. Where was he going with this?

"He would be an incredibly young-looking thirty-eight," one of them finally replied.

"But it's possible," the second added.

"How about if I told you he was in his late eighties?"

They both laughed nervously and looked even more uneasy. "No, sir, that would not be believable."

"It's good to know that you do not believe this young man is in his eighties, because if you had taken the time to actually *read* the alert, you would have noted that the person of interest who was flagged is in fact in his nineties," he said.

The two of them exchanged accusing looks, as if the other was to blame.

"I think the two of you should leave now," he said, "but before you do, you owe this young man an apology."

"We're terribly sorry," one mumbled.

"Yes, terribly."

The man smiled. "Actually, you will be much sorrier after we discuss my displeasure at being called down here on a wild-goose chase. You should now leave, but please, gentlemen, don't go too far. We *will* be chatting."

They bumped into each other as they scrambled to get out of the room, closing the door behind them.

The remaining man walked over, took the chair from the corner, placed it across from me and sat. His expression softened for the first time.

"I would like to formally offer apologies from the British government for what has just transpired."

"Thanks...it's okay."

"It is not okay. It is a rather sad testament to the quality of junior officers we are able to recruit.

Perhaps the ability to read and do simple mathematics should be requirements for admission to the section."

"What does 'section' mean?" I asked.

He smiled again. "We're all just employees of the Queen. I'd like to explain what happened. Your passport triggered an alert, which requires a secondary inspection. All very common. What is uncommon is that those two—shall we say—gentlemen failed to follow any semblance of protocol, including something as simple as verifying your age." He paused. "You are not an incredibly well-preserved ninety-three-year-old, are you?"

"Of course not!"

He chuckled. "Just checking. It is unfortunate that you share the same Canadian passport and exact name of a person who is of interest to us."

I almost said, "I'm named after my grandfather" but stopped myself. I had a terrible thought. "Somebody who is in his nineties, right?"

"If not already dead."

"Yeah, he probably would be," I said.

"I really think they need to update our alerts. Even if this David McLean was alive, I can't imagine he would still present a threat to national security."

"I guess not. Can I go now? I have somebody waiting for me."

"Certainly." He reached down and picked up my bag and handed it to me.

"Thank you, sir."

"I appreciate your being so understanding. I'd like to make sure this doesn't happen again on your exit from our country."

"This could happen again?" I gasped.

"Let's just make sure that if it does, it can be quickly rectified. Take my card." He reached in and pulled out his wallet. I couldn't be certain, but I thought I caught a glimpse of a holster holding a pistol. He removed a business card and handed it to me.

I took the card. It was simple—white with black lettering: *Justin Bourne—British Government.*

"Justin *Bourne*?" I asked.

"Yes, like the movies. Thank goodness my parents didn't name me Jason...although it would be rather brilliant to be a secret agent—at least I would imagine."

"What is it that you actually do?" I asked.

"As it says on the card, I am simply an employee of the government. You'd best not keep Doris waiting."

I stood up and then stopped. "Wait, how did *they* know—how do *you* know—that Doris is picking me up?" I asked.

"Believe me, it's not because of any intelligence coup. They went out to the waiting area and found somebody who was in fact waiting for you. It's important that you hang onto that card, very important, unless you want this to be repeated, perhaps, when you try to leave the country. It could end in a much less pleasant manner."

"I'll take good care of it," I said. I tucked it into my pocket.

"Now if you'll excuse me, I have other matters to attend to."

He turned on his heels and quickly walked out of the room, the door closing behind him with a thud, leaving me alone. Alone felt very good.

FOUR

I was alone and free to leave. Now I just had to go. I put my beret back on, turned the door handle gently and was relieved when the door opened, and then even more relieved to see an empty corridor stretching out in front of me and neither of the twins waiting for me. I had the feeling they weren't too pleased with me, and I didn't want to give them another chance to have me do anything the hard way. If they'd had time to search my bag, I wouldn't be walking anywhere; instead of them being in trouble, it would have been me.

I looked up and down the corridor. In one direction—the way I'd been frog-marched—was a door that said *DO NOT ENTER* in bold letters. I decided to go through the unmarked door at the other end. It was unlocked, and I slowly pushed it open and peered out. There were passengers, luggage in tow, flowing in one direction toward an exit. An exit was what I needed. I threw my bag over my shoulder and joined the horde of passengers exiting the terminal. I had the sensation of being part of a herd where I could hide from anybody who might want to pull me into a private room.

The big double doors slid open to reveal a semicircle of people waiting and watching for the passenger that belonged to them. I scanned the crowd for Doris. I didn't see her. There were so many people. A number of them held up signs with names; obviously, whoever they were meeting was a stranger to them. I caught sight of a crudely made sign that read *McLean.* It certainly wasn't Doris holding it; the guy wasn't much older than me. He was dressed in sort of a retro-style suit and had a fedora on his head. It was strange that my name, which wasn't common, had come up twice since I'd landed.

I walked the length of the crowd, looking for Doris, without any luck. The two scary agents had obviously talked to her, so she must know that I'd landed, and I knew she was in the terminal somewhere. But she didn't seem to be here now. Had she gone to the washroom or a restaurant, or had she gotten tired and found somewhere to sit down? No, Doris had climbed Kilimanjaro, so waiting at an airport for an hour wasn't going to tire her out. It was almost embarrassing to think about the climb and realize that I wouldn't have made it to the top without her.

I walked back along the line. I must have missed her. I went up to the guy holding the sign with my name on it. "That's my name," I said casually.

"If you are DJ, it is wonderful that you recognized it." He spoke with a very upper-class British accent.

"I am, but you're not Doris."

"My grandmother said you were *very* bright, so I'm not surprised in the least that you can tell that I am not she."

Did he just take a shot at me? Best to ignore it. "Doris is your grandmother?"

"Again, a fine demonstration of your powers of observation. You would impress Sherlock Holmes himself with such deductive reasoning."

Before I could respond, he turned on his heel and walked away. I pushed and dodged through the crowd and caught up to him as he exited the terminal. It was cool and raining outside, although we were sheltered under a roof.

"I was expecting Doris, is all," I explained.

"I was expecting to be out with my friends, so some things don't work out as we desire. And to top it off, you were terribly tardy."

"Sorry, but it wasn't like it was my idea to be detained for questioning."

"I imagine your delay is related to those two men who came and talked to me. They saw me with the sign and approached me. I told them I was a stand-in for my grandmother. They were more than a little frightening and tried their best to be intimidating," he said.

"You should have spent time with them alone in a locked room if you want to know what scary is."

"Were they MI5?"

"What?" I asked.

"British Security Service," he explained.

"They didn't tell me anything, including their names."

"And what exactly did you do to bring them down upon you?" he asked.

"I didn't do anything. It was just a case of mistaken identity."

"Isn't that what every criminal says? Or perhaps they found your beret so questionable they had to—"

I grabbed him by the arm and spun him around so that we were eye to eye—although his eyes were a bit lower than mine. "This beret belonged to my grandfather. He wore it until he died. He left it for me. I wear it in his honor. Is there anything else you'd like to say about it before we go any further?"

He looked shocked and more than a little shaken. Those two men weren't the only ones who could be intimidating.

"Because my keen powers of observation tell me I'm a lot bigger than you," I added.

"Are you threatening me?" he stuttered.

"I guess I'm not the only one who's observant, although technically I'm not threatening you," I said—although I guess I was. Maybe it wasn't such a wise thing to beat up my friend's grandson. He was a jerk, but she probably loved him.

I released my grip on his arm and he straightened his shirt and jacket, which had gotten sort of rumpled in my hands.

"I'm sorry. How about if we start over?" I reached out my hand. "My name is David and I'm pleased to meet you."

He held out his hand and we shook. "Charles." That was better. "Now climb in." He pointed at a green MGB sports car parked at the curb. There was a large yellow ticket on the windshield, held in place by the wiper. He took it, ripped it in two and dropped it on the pavement.

"That's your car?"

"Again, a brilliant observation."

I had a further desire to pop him as he took my bag from me, but bringing a bleeding grandson home would not be the greatest greeting. I walked around the car, opened the right passenger door and there was a steering wheel staring at me. England—wrong side of the car, wrong side of the road.

"Unless you're planning on driving, I suggest you climb in the other side," Charles said.

So much for us starting over. All I wanted to do was drive him—one good shot to the jaw. How could somebody as nice as Doris have a grandson who so desperately needed a kick in the butt? We both climbed in, he started the engine, and we drove away.

"Why didn't your grandmother come to pick me up?"

"She had a slight accident."

"Is she all right?" I exclaimed.

"Not right enough to pick you up, but she'll be fine."

"What happened?" I asked.

"I'll let her tell the story."

I wanted to press further but knew there was little point.

We turned onto a street hardly wide enough for one car but with two-way traffic. The narrow street was lined by brick, three-story row houses. It felt a bit like driving into a canyon.

"Here we are," Charles said as we came to a stop.

"Thanks for the ride. I really appreciated it," I said as I climbed out of the car, bag in hand.

"I'm sure you did."

He started to pull away from the curb before I'd even closed the door!

"Wait, which house is it?" I yelled.

"Two twenty-one!" he yelled back. He reached over, pulled the door shut and drove off, leaving me in a bluish cloud of exhaust.

"Glad I could help...my pleasure...is there anything else I can do...so nice to meet you," I muttered to myself, thinking of all the possible responses he could have given.

I looked for the address. There it was, right across the street. I looked to the left, stepped into the street and heard a loud honk and the squeal of brakes. I jumped back onto the curb. A taxi had skidded to a stop. I'd forgotten to look in the *right* direction: to the right.

"Watch yourself, you bloody idiot!" the driver called out of his window as he slowly drove by.

So much for English hospitality. In the short time I'd been in England, I'd been detained by government agents, threatened with a full cavity search, been practically dumped at the side of the road and now had almost been run over. At least the guy in the taxi had reason to be annoyed at me.

It would have been an incredibly bad way to end this adventure—hit by taxi on the streets of London. How would I explain that to my mother? How would I explain any of this?

I looked to the right—and to the left—and proceeded safely across the street and up the stairs of 221. It was a nice-looking home, almost identical to the rest of the houses up and down the street. I rang the bell and it sounded out loud and clear. I waited. No answer. I waited a few more beats, so I wouldn't be rude, and then rang again. There was still no answer. Did I mishear the number? Did he say 221 or something else? Would I have to go door to door to find Doris? Surely some of her neighbors would know her even if this wasn't the right house.

I started to walk away and then turned back. I reached out and turned the doorknob. The door was unlocked. I opened it slowly and poked my head inside. Overhead was a big crystal chandelier, and on the floor was an ornate carpet. The walls were adorned with paintings, and there was a dark wooden table with a big gold-framed mirror above it. I don't know much about home décor, but I do know when things look expensive.

"Hello!" I called out, my voice echoing down the hallway. I was starting to think this wasn't such a smart idea, that I should close the door and retreat before anybody called the police on me.

"DJ, is that you?" a faint voice answered.

"Yes! Doris?"

"I'm up here...upstairs!"

There was a flight of stairs at the end of the hall. I raced to it, almost tripping on the rug, and then took the stairs two and three at a time. And there she was, in a big comfy chair with her leg up on a stool and a big white cast on her leg! I rushed over and threw my arms around her and gave her a big hug. I felt happy and relieved and confused.

"It is so wonderful to see you, dear boy!" she said, beaming. "Now, let me have a look at you!"

I straightened up.

"I do believe you have grown since I last saw you. Perhaps not taller but thicker, stronger-looking."

"I've been doing a lot of weight training for football, so I've added fifteen pounds of muscle."

"It shows. And I'm so happy to see you wearing the beret. It looks like it belongs up there!"

I reached up and touched it. "Your grandson commented on it as well." I decided not to repeat what he had said.

"And where is my grandson?"

"He seemed to be in a hurry. I thanked him and he was gone. He mentioned you'd had an accident but wouldn't tell me what happened. So...what happened?"

"I tripped on one of my cats."

"Really?"

She laughed. "I climbed Kilimanjaro, and I was felled by a tabby. It happened only last night."

"Is it bad? Does it hurt?"

"It's a little sore, but nothing I can't live with. I'm afraid it's my pride that was damaged as much as my leg. Please, come and have a seat."

I sat down in a big chair across from her. I looked around. This room was as fancy as the hall.

"You have a beautiful home," I said.

"It's most comfortable. I've thought about moving. It's a bit big for just one old woman to ramble around in."

"You climbed Kilimanjaro, so you're not that old."

"Sweet of you to say, but it may be time to move. Thank goodness I have my housekeeper and cook to help me."

"Wow, servants," I said without thinking.

"Just part-time, but very essential right now to take care of me. My dear husband left me very comfortable," she said. "He was, as they say, *active* in government circles."

He must have been *very* active to afford a house like this.

"I'm just so sorry that this has happened now, and I won't be able to ferry you around London and show you the sights."

"Don't worry about that. I can get myself around, no problem."

"I'm sure you can, but what sort of a host would I be if I left you to your own devices?" she asked. "I've arranged for Charlie to take you around."

"And *Charlie* agreed?" I asked, feeling very surprised. He didn't seem much like a Charlie or very agreeable.

"Right away. I'm sure the two of you will get on brilliantly."

And I was sure if Doris had been along for the car ride, she would have thought different.

"You will get to see the London Eye, the museums, Buckingham Palace, the changing of the guard—perhaps even have a night out. You will be here for New Year's Eve, correct?"

"I'm not scheduled to head back until the third."

"I think Charlie is planning on taking in the celebration in Trafalgar Square," she said. "It's the English version of Times Square."

"That's really not necessary." Or possible, if I was relying on Charlie to befriend me.

"It is, unless you want to bring in the New Year sipping tea with an old woman with a broken leg."

"I can think of worse ways to celebrate," I replied.

"Then you have a far better imagination than I possess." She paused. "So tell me, not that I'm not thrilled to have you here, what prompted this very impulsive decision to come to London?"

I had tried to rehearse this moment in my head without success. Explaining to Doris why I was here was going to be only slightly easier than explaining it to my mother when I got home.

"You're going to think this is crazy."

"I'm British. We thrive on outlandish thinking, eccentric ideas and people. Please."

I pulled the papers out of my jacket pocket and handed them to her. "These are from a notebook my grandfather kept. It was hidden; my cousins and I discovered it by accident."

She studied the pages one after the other and then looked up at me. "This appears to be in code."

I nodded.

"And you're sure it's his doing, that this is his writing?"

"Positive."

"That means one of two things. Either he was a little off his rocker or he was a spy."

FIVE

In one quick burst I told her everything: the money, the disguises, the loaded Walther PPK and, of course, the passports. I didn't mention the bag of golf balls because, well, it seemed too bizarre and not to the point.

"I have two of the passports with me," I said. I dug down into my bag, pulled them out and handed them to her.

She opened both to the identification page. "Your grandfather was certainly a handsome young man in his younger days."

"He claimed he was still a handsome man in his *older* days."

"I can certainly see the family resemblance," she said.

"People have always said I look like him, but I could never see it until recently. My mother says I'm growing into him."

"Particularly in this picture—this could be an older you." She held the Spanish passport up. My grandfather had a beard and mustache in that picture.

I still only saw my grandfather, but maybe there was some resemblance around the eyes. If I had a beard and mustache—if I could grow any facial hair beyond a dark smudge over my mouth—I might have been able to use that passport.

"I don't know about the Spanish passport, but I'm certain this UK passport is real," she said.

"Are you trying to tell me my grandfather's name is really Nigel Finch?" I asked.

"Well, probably not."

"Definitely not!" I said. "He lived his whole life as David McLean."

"There have been recorded cases of people living under false identities for scores of years, either given a new name for protective reasons or because they are deep sleepers."

I wanted to ask what a deep sleeper was, but this was all going in too crazy a direction. My grandfather was David McLean, not somebody named Nigel Finch...or Pedro Martinez.

"Please believe me, I'm not saying that his name was Nigel, only that the actual passport is genuine stock. You need government contacts to obtain these." She held it up to the light and scratched at it with her fingernail. "And this is certainly a very good forgery. I'm very impressed."

"I don't think the people at Passport Control would have been so impressed. That's why I was late. I was pulled over for extra inspection."

"Why would they do that?"

"They said my passport lit up their system like a Christmas tree, but before they started searching me or my bag, they discovered that they were looking for another David McLean." I paused. "Somebody my grandfather's age."

"Ah, the plot thickens. So your grandfather is somehow known to the UK Border Agency."

"Or somebody else with the same name," I said.

"Perhaps. Tell me, what did your grandfather do for a living before he retired?"

"He was in the import/export business." I thought back to Adam saying that was a great cover for a spy.

"So I imagine he traveled a great deal," Doris said.

"He'd retired before I was born, but I guess so."

What I didn't mention was that after he'd retired, he'd still traveled all around the world to play golf. I knew where this conversation was going.

"And did he speak multiple languages, by any chance?"

"Not well, but he did speak some German and French...and Spanish."

"And how did your grandfather feel about weapons, guns and such?" Doris asked.

"He *hated* them. He said nobody but police officers and the military should carry weapons."

"The lady doth protest too much methinks," Doris said.

Now she'd lost me completely.

"It's a line from Shakespeare's *Hamlet*, spoken by Queen Gertrude. It means that she doubted the truth of a statement because it was so vehemently denied."

I understood her knowing Shakespeare, but I had one other question. "So how do you know all these things about spies?" I asked.

"I love a good espionage novel—and didn't you notice my address?" she asked.

"Um...221...right?"

"Yes. We're only missing the *B* for this to be Sherlock Holmes's address. My husband insisted we purchase our home based on the address. We were both fanatical Baker Street Irregulars."

I put my head in my hands. This was all moving too fast.

"I understand this is hard to take in, but you must believe some of what I'm saying. After all, you wouldn't have suddenly come here if you didn't already suspect something," Doris said.

I shook my head. "That is a good deduction."

"Thank you, Watson."

"I suspect something, but I don't believe he was James Bond," I said.

"Nobody is saying that he wore a tuxedo, drove around in an Aston Martin and drank martinis—shaken, not stirred."

"My grandfather hardly drank, ever."

"Most agents don't drink. They need to be in constant control of their faculties. Believe me, I'm not saying that he was a James Bond-type agent. That isn't what most agents are like. Most of them are private citizens enlisted by the government to observe and make note of specific things in the countries in which they travel. They use their contacts to bring materials into and out of certain countries, crossing borders and delivering messages to other agents. Do you think your grandfather could have been involved in those kinds of activities?"

"Yeah, he could have been doing those things."

"Now if we could only make sense of what is written here," she said, tapping the sheets of paper.

"All I know is, it involves England and, specifically, Cambridge. I spent the whole flight staring at it, but it seemed to make less sense the more I looked at it."

"Did you sleep at all?"

"I basically haven't slept since all this started. I was hoping it would begin to make sense once I got here."

"Often, things make greater sense after a good night's sleep. You must be exhausted."

"It would be good if I could lie down for a bit." I picked up the passports and went to take the notebook pages. Doris stopped me.

"Let me have a look at them. Fresh eyes might be the solution. I've had the guest room at the end of the hall made up for you," Doris said. "It has fresh sheets, already turned down by the maid. Just go to sleep."

"Thanks."

I stood and picked up my bag. It felt heavy. My legs felt heavy. My head felt heavy. How could any of this be true? I trudged to the guest room and flopped down on the bed. The springs groaned loudly. I should have changed or washed up or even taken off my shoes, but I was just too tired. My body was exhausted, but my mind was still spinning. Nigel Finch...if that was really his name, then if I was named after him I'd be Nigel instead of David. I closed my eyes. I wondered if I would dream David's dreams or Nigel's?

I heard loud voices arguing and opened my eyes. It was dark, but there was enough light coming in through the window for me to see that I was someplace unfamiliar. Then it came back—I was in London, at Doris's home. I looked at my watch, pushing the little button to light the dial. It glowed green. It was three in the afternoon, so why was it dark out? Okay, it was three in the afternoon at home; here, it was...six hours' difference...it was nine, so it made sense that it was dark outside.

I got out of bed and opened the door; the voices got louder. There were a lot of them, and they weren't arguing so much as having a noisy discussion. I went down the corridor and was greeted by the sight of a bunch of old people—older people—in the living room. Doris seemed to be at the very center of the group.

"This makes no bloody sense," one man exclaimed, his voice rising above the din of the others.

He was dressed in a strange hat like the one Sherlock Holmes wore in the old movies. He lifted up his hand—he was holding a page from Grandpa's notebook.

"This is rubbish!" he said as he ripped the sheet in two and dropped the pieces to the floor.

"What are you doing?" I exclaimed. I practically jumped across the room, dropped to my knees and grabbed the torn halves. I was so shocked, I didn't know what to say.

"Don't worry. I have the original right here," Doris said. She held up a sheet and turned it to show me. "I made copies," she explained. "We're all working on copies. Let me introduce my friends and fellow Holmesians."

"Holmesians?" I asked.

"We belong to a Sherlock Holmes club," the man in the odd hat said. "We gather on a monthly basis to discuss all things Sherlock Holmes."

"And I couldn't think of any other group who would be more able to break this code," Doris said.

"Well, short of Sherlock and Watson," a woman said, and they all laughed politely.

"Our illustrious group includes a mathematics professor."

The man who had torn up the sheets tipped his hat at me.

"An international chess grand master."

"Charmed," an older woman said.

"A children's writer."

Another woman greeted me with a smile.

"And a former military encryption officer."

"Retired," he said. He gave a two-fingered salute. With his short hair and thick mustache, he still looked like a military man.

"I guess from what I've heard you haven't broken the code yet," I said.

Doris shook her head.

"We've made a basic assumption that it is a substitution formula where the numbers and letters on the page represent another number or letter," the mathematics professor explained.

"The difficulty is discovering the transposition key," Doris added.

"And believe me, we've applied very advanced applications to this task. We've used a dozen of the most complex cipher formulas, but have not been able to provide a successful translation," he added.

"But we are completely confident that we can break the code," the military officer said. "It's all just a matter of time."

"How much time?" I asked.

"I'd say no longer than two weeks at the most."

"But I don't have that long. I'm only here for a few days," I explained.

"Perhaps I can convince an old colleague to allow me to borrow the supercomputer at Oxford," the professor said.

"That would be brilliant!" Doris beamed.

"And most helpful. It's just that this code was obviously written by a person with expertise in encryption."

"My grandfather wrote it," I said. "But I don't think he was really an expert." Then again, what did I know?

"With the holiday break, it is more likely that the computer will be sitting idle, so we might be able to nab some time, especially if we go in the middle of the night," the professor said.

"Of course, with a code of this complexity, it might take even a supercomputer over an hour to run all the variables."

"I wonder," the chess master said. "English is not my first language—or even my second or third—so can somebody tell me which word is most common in your language?"

"The," three of them said at once.

"And the most common letters?" she asked.

"I believe it is the vowel *e*, followed by the consonant *t* and then the vowel *a*," the military man said.

They all started to chuckle. It was like a light had gone on for all of them simultaneously.

"We're looking for something complex when the answer was hiding in plain sight!" Doris exclaimed.

"This is child's play!" another snorted.

"It's actually genius to make it so simple!"

"You can decode it?" I asked.

"DJ, if what we're all thinking is right, a clever five-year-old could decode it," Doris said. "Now let's see if we're right."

SIX

Doris frantically began cleaning off a chalkboard in the corner of the room, balancing precariously on her crutches. I hadn't even noticed the board before. Once it was wiped clean, she picked up a piece of chalk and wrote the word *Cambridge.* Then the others began calling out letters to her. I watched in fascination as the words started to appear.

Six not Five
Apostles
Haigha knows the truth

It all makes sense through the looking glass
Zzzzz zzzzz zzzzz zzzzz zzzzz
Stanley Homer Hicks Johnson Liszt Birdie Amoeba

I saw the words, but how did any of this make sense? What were the Apostles, and who were those six people? What did five sets of five *z*'s mean? And an amoeba? Was that even how it was spelled? And finally, who was Haigha, because if he knew the truth, he was the person I really needed to talk to—forget about Stanley and Homer and the others.

"Does any of this make sense to anybody?" I asked.

They all shook their heads. "Well, not yet, but we've converted the first part…at least I hope we have. Now we need to convert the numbers at the bottom of the page to letters."

"I'm going to make a basic assumption that if the numbers became letters that by applying the same formula we can make the numbers into letters," Doris said.

I read out the groups of letters, and they were converted and written down as numbers.

7028*3675*02

7312*1694*02

982*763*3221

05824*33956

827*9532*161

894962*8091

"Is that it?" Doris asked.

"That's all of them," I said.

They all crowded around, staring at the chalkboard, silent, studying. I moved in close as well and looked over Doris's head to see the board. I could read the words, but that didn't mean that any of it made any sense to me. I shifted anxiously from foot to foot, waiting for somebody to have a eureka moment and explain it all, but we continued to stand in silence—a silence that was making me increasingly uncomfortable. Finally I spoke.

"So what does this all mean?"

They exchanged questioning looks. "I haven't the faintest notion," the military man said.

"It's gibberish to me," the chess master said.

"Well, I do see one connection," the professor offered, and we all turned to him.

"The reference to Cambridge is the obvious clue that was not coded," he said.

"That's what brought me here to England—the reference to Cambridge," I said.

"And the word beneath it is *Apostles.* There is a little-known discussion group of Cambridge graduates who refer to themselves as the Apostles."

"Either a definite clue or a strange coincidence," Doris said.

"We in the encryption game don't believe in coincidences," the military man said. "It must mean something. Perhaps those names are members of that club."

"And how would we find that out?" I asked.

"It's a rather secretive club, but they do have a diary which they simply call *the book*. Members' names are recorded there."

"How can I read the book?"

He shook his head. "I don't think you can unless you are a member of the club…or know a member of the club." He smiled. "And I know a member. I'll make arrangements for you to go up to Cambridge and meet with him."

"Excellent!" Doris said. "I'll arrange for Charlie to take DJ to Cambridge."

I was pretty sure Charlie wouldn't find it excellent, but for my part, beggars couldn't be choosers—I'd ride along with good old Charlie. "Great. Thanks, everybody."

"And now I will make a copy of the decoded words for everybody and send you all home to think and to look at it afresh in the morning," Doris said.

"Would you mind if we shared it with other people?" the military man asked. "You know, other experts in decryption or mysteries, perhaps other Holmesian societies?"

Doris looked at me. "They say many hands make light work."

I shrugged. "Sure, share away."

I lay in bed, fighting to keep my eyes open. There was one more thing I needed to do. I pulled out my phone to text Steve.

`Hope things are going well. We broke the code–sort of–and it might work for your entries as well. Frequency of letters. 1 = e, 2 = t, 3 = a, 4 = o You get the idea. Look up the rest. Gotta sleep. Good luck.`

SEVEN

DECEMBER 29

"Would you like a little more tea?" the maid, Gladys, asked.

"Yes, please."

She poured tea into my cup, which was made of very light, almost paper-thin china. I felt big and clumsy, afraid that I'd crush it in my grip. I already felt more than a little self-conscious about the orange marmalade I'd spilled on the expensive-looking white linen tablecloth. Right after I'd done that, Doris had dripped some on it as well, and I thought she had done it on purpose to make me feel better. It actually did make me feel better, because it was such a kind thing to do. It was the act of a gracious person—just like she'd been on the mountain, when her spirit practically carried me to the top.

I felt good. I had a solid night's sleep under my belt and I was ready to try to figure things out—although so far, I hadn't been able to figure out anything.

"Did you have any more thoughts about what the messages mean?" I asked.

"The reference to *through the looking glass* refers to the classic story by Lewis Carroll, of course, and Haigha is the rabbit that Alice encounters."

"Sort of like the March Hare in *Alice in Wonderland*."

"They are one and the same," Doris said. "I'm going to go through the book today, word by word, and try to see if there is a clue that will unlock the other decoded words."

"Do you want me to look through the book too?"

"I don't think that is necessary. I will have a great deal of help from my fellow Holmesians. As we suggested, with your permission we've cast the net wider and asked other clubs to weigh in on what they think the messages mean."

"That can only help," I said.

"So while we're wrestling with the riddles, you need to proceed to Cambridge."

"I just wish we had more to go on before I head up there."

"The worst that will happen is that you and Charlie have a wonderful trip up to Cambridge together."

"I'm sure," I said. Driving up with Charlie was going to be anything but wonderful. I was just hoping he wouldn't push me to do something we'd both regret. "How long is the drive?"

"It's not much more than an hour if you take the motorway, but I hope you'll take the back roads and enjoy the drive. That was the way my husband and I always traveled. It's so much lovelier to take the back routes."

I was hoping for speed, and I was sure that would suit her grandson as well. The less time we had together the better, as far as I was concerned.

"I know the two of you will get along famously. Don't tell anybody, but while I love all my grandchildren equally, I really *adore* Charlie...such spirit... such *joie de vivre*...and, I'm sure you'll agree, rather striking."

I didn't even know how to answer her. I smiled and gave a slight nod of my head. I couldn't help but wonder what Doris's other grandchildren were like if Charlie was the one she liked the best.

"I'm going to let you take my vehicle," Doris said.

"But doesn't Charlie have a vehicle?" I wondered if he'd borrowed the vehicle he drove in from the airport.

"I'm afraid Charlie isn't much of a driver. I'd prefer if you drove." She pulled out some keys and handed them to me. I hesitated to take them. "You do drive, correct?"

"Definitely...but on the right-hand side of the road."

"So now you sit on the right-hand side of the *car* and drive on the left-hand side of the *road*. Simple. Just watch the other cars."

I took the keys.

"I'm surprised Charlie isn't here by now," Doris said.

I was more surprised he'd agreed to come in the first place and still wondered if he'd show at all. Either way, I now had a car and could get there on my own if I had to. It might be better if he didn't show.

The doorbell warbled, and I could hear the maid going to answer it. Then the door opened and I heard voices. Good old Charlie was here.

Gladys walked into the dining room, followed by a girl about my age—a *beautiful* girl.

"Hello, Nana!" the girl exclaimed as she threw her arms around Doris.

"So wonderful to see you, my darling," Doris replied.

My mouth dropped open. I didn't know who she was or how she knew Doris, but I did know she was stunning—curvy in all the right places, with long blond hair and, I saw as she turned to face me, startling blue eyes. I had to fight not to look away.

"DJ, I'd like you to meet my granddaughter, Charlie."

She reached out a hand to shake mine.

"You're Charlie?" I gasped.

"Short for Charlotte," she said. She still had her hand extended.

I recovered enough to awkwardly grab her hand and shake. "I just wasn't expecting you...when Doris...your grandmother said Charlie, I thought she meant Charles."

"My cousin?" Charlie asked.

"Yes, he drove me in from the airport."

"That must have been a *real* pleasure," Charlie said. She gave me a questioning look, and I realized I was still clinging to her hand. Embarrassed, I let it go. My hand was damp with sweat.

"Do you remember on the mountain I told you that I wanted you to meet one of my granddaughters?" Doris asked. "Well, this is the one. Isn't she beautiful?"

I wasn't sure how I was supposed to answer that.

"Nana, you're embarrassing DJ and me. Please, I don't think he came all this way to be set up."

"No, I mean yes—I mean, yes, she is beautiful and...this is embarrassing." I looked away. I was sure I was blushing.

Charlie sat down and Doris poured her a cup of tea.

"So, my darling, do you have any commitments today or are you totally free?" Doris asked her granddaughter.

"I'm as free as a bird for the holidays. My next shoot isn't until January second."

"Shoot?" I asked. "Are you a photographer?"

"Oh, goodness, she's on the other side of the lens, DJ!" Doris exclaimed. "She's one of the most—"

"Nana, please," Charlie said, cutting her off. "I am a photographer, but for this shoot I'm afraid I'm on the *wrong* side of the lens. It's so much more interesting to point the camera than have it pointed at you."

"So you have the whole day free for the trip up to Cambridge with DJ?" Doris asked.

"Certainly, although I thought I was going to be showing him the sights of London, not a dusty university campus."

"Perhaps that could be tonight or even tomorrow, but he has an errand to run in Cambridge first."

I looked to see if there was a trace of annoyance in her face about having to babysit me. If there was, I didn't see it. All I saw was, well, those startling blue eyes set against flawless skin and a perfect little upturned nose and—

"Then it's settled. You're off to Cambridge!"

I was feeling more than a little self-conscious. Charlie wasn't just beautiful, but beautiful in a way that was almost unnerving. I'd had girlfriends, some of them really, really pretty, but she was a cut above pretty. I had to stop myself from staring at her as we headed for the garage to get the car. Thank goodness she was leading and didn't know I was looking at her.

"My nana really likes you," she said as she spun around.

"I like her too," I said, embarrassed that she'd caught me staring.

"She's always going on about the mountain and how you helped her to the top."

"Believe me, she helped me as much as I helped her."

"Now you're just being sweet and chivalrous."

I wasn't, but I'd take the compliment. I really wouldn't have made it to the top without Doris. I hated to admit it, even to myself, but in the beginning I'd been upset there was an "old" woman in our party—I thought she would just slow me down. I guess in some ways she did—she slowed me down enough to make it to the top. Both my grandmothers died before I was old enough to know them. I like to think they were as wonderful as Doris.

"Nana must *really* trust you."

"I guess she does."

"No guessing involved. Here's the proof." She opened up the big sliding garage door to reveal the car. It was bright red, a convertible, and the hood seemed to go on forever and ever.

"It's...it's a *Jaguar*," I stammered.

"Not just a Jaguar. It's a Jag E-Type. Twelve cylinders, capable of going a hundred and seventy-five miles per hour and accelerating from zero to sixty in slightly under five seconds."

"I'm impressed...by the car and your knowledge." I ran my hand along the hood. Most cars now only had four or six cylinders, but there were twelve trapped under there. It was a beast.

"This is considered the most beautiful car ever designed. One was purchased by the New York Museum of Modern Art, so it is the only car ever formally called a work of art by an institution." She turned to me, and I looked up from the car. Thank goodness she hadn't caught me staring at her again.

"How much is this thing worth?" I asked.

"It's hard to put a price on something this exquisite and unique, but you couldn't replace it for under seventy thousand pounds."

I did a rough conversion in my head. That was about $130,000.

"I've never even sat in anything worth that much," I said.

"And now you have the keys to it in your hand, so I think it's fair to assume that Nana trusts you very, very much. Get in."

I walked down the side of the car and pulled open the door.

"You realize that the wheel is on the other side," she said.

I'd forgotten. Again. I looked like an idiot in front of her. A great start needed a better recovery. "And you realize that a gentleman should always hold the door open for a lady," I said.

She smiled—a beautiful, knee-melting smile—but had she bought it?

She slipped into the seat and I gently closed the door behind her. I circled around—it was a long, long way around that hood and those cylinders—

and climbed in, and down, beside her. The car was very low, and from the driver's seat, the hood seemed even longer. I inserted the key, and the engine started with a low, powerful rumble, refinement disguising the power I knew was there.

"I assume you've never driven a Jag before, correct?" Charlie asked.

"I've never even been in one before."

"Have you ever driven on our side of the road?"

I shook my head.

"This could be interesting. Most people have trouble with the right-hand turn—they turn into oncoming traffic. Just remember that the driver is always in the center of the road and you'll be fine."

I put the car into gear, grateful it was an automatic. Working a stick with my left hand would have been an even bigger complication. Slowly I eased out of the garage, making sure that it was clear on both sides. I turned to the right, going wide so that I was in the center and the car was on the "wrong" side of the road.

"Do you know how to get to Cambridge?" I asked.

"I can navigate as long as you can drive. Let's head for the motorway."

"But Doris suggested the back roads."

She shook her head. "Aren't you curious to see how fast this car can go?"

"A little," I admitted.

"Well, we can't really find out how fast this thing can move along any country roads. Onward to the highway!"

I turned onto the ramp and started along the motorway. The car responded instantly to the touch of my foot, and we gathered speed. The lane ahead was clear, and I used the side mirror to ease into traffic, settling in behind a truck. The engine purred, and the ride was soft and smooth. I was enjoying this.

"You know, just because this is my grandmother's car, you don't have to drive it like you're my grandmother," Charlie said.

Carefully looking in my side and rearview mirrors, I put on my turn signal and changed lanes.

"I can see why she trusts you. You do drive like her. It seems a shame to waste such a fine piece of—"

I put my foot down, the engine raced, and we jumped forward like the car had been stung by a bee, snapping Charlie's head back against the headrest.

"Is that a little better?" I asked.

We raced past a truck like it had suddenly been thrown into reverse and came up quickly on the cars in the lane ahead. I switched lanes again, still carefully but not as obviously so, and moved into the passing lane.

"What's the speed limit on this highway?" I asked.

"There didn't even used to be speed limits on the motorways, but now it's seventy miles an hour."

I looked down at the speedometer. I was doing almost ninety-five! I hit the brakes—hard—and we slowed down dramatically and moved back into the middle lane and then the driving lane at the far left.

"So are you disappointed you have to spend this time with me instead of my cousin Charles?"

"It's pretty much a toss-up. I can hardly tell one of you from the other," I said.

She laughed. "So do you think I'm a git too?" she demanded.

"I don't even know what a git is."

"If you've spent time with Charles, you know exactly what a git is! It means annoying, stupid, incompetent, childish. The sort of person you want to throttle."

"I was thinking more along the lines of popping him."

She looked confused. "You wanted to give him a soda?"

"It means punching him. I wanted to punch him," I explained.

"If you ever do that, please let me know. I think I could sell tickets for that. That boy is all mouth and no trousers."

"Okay, now you're confusing me again," I said.

"That means all talk and no action. He's nothing but a blowhard."

"I guess we don't always use the same words to mean the same thing," I said.

"George Bernard Shaw said that England and America are two countries divided by a common language."

"I'm not American."

"American, Canadian…it's all the same to us," she said.

"I understand why you Irish would think that."

"I'm not Irish, I'm...okay, point taken, Mr. Canada."

As we talked, I carefully changed lanes and maneuvered around slower vehicles. I didn't want to be accused of being a grandmother again, although I was going to do it without reaching warp speed. It would have been something to drive this car where there weren't any speed limits.

"So tell me a little bit about this mission you're on," Charlie said.

"It's a little hard to explain, but I can show you when we stop. I have some notebook pages in my jacket pocket." I wanted both hands firmly on the wheel.

"No need to stop." She reached over and started digging in my jacket pockets.

"I'm really ticklish!" I exclaimed as I squirmed in my seat.

"That's something for me to file away, perhaps for a later time."

It felt like my whole body flushed. She pulled out the pages and unfolded them. I watched her out of the corner of my eye as she read them.

Finally she spoke. "This is what brought you across the pond?" she asked.

"That and the other things we found. Some passports, money, an escape kit and a gun."

"You didn't bring the gun with you, did you?"

"Of course not."

"Good. We're pretty strict about weapons in this country. So what are you hoping to find?" she asked.

"I guess who or what my grandfather really was. It's not just me. My cousins are investigating other notebook entries, trying to find out answers too."

"And talking to this man in Cambridge will give you the answer?" Charlie asked.

"It's all I've got to go on so—"

Her phone began to ring. "Excuse me," she said. "Hello…oh, *hi*!"

She turned slightly away.

"I'm on my way up to Cambridge…yes…with nobody."

Nobody? I was a nobody?

"Yes, I'm looking forward to it too. It should be a wonderful way to bring in the New Year together."

Was she talking to a girlfriend? No, the tone of voice left little doubt: she was talking to a guy she liked.

I pulled out to pass another truck, and the car behind me pulled out as well. That was the fourth time it had followed me when I passed another car; each time, it settled back in not directly behind me, but a car or even two cars back.

I accelerated, going faster than the limit, and passed a second and then a third truck. The car—it looked like a BMW—kept pace with me. There was another truck I could pass, but I decided not to. I went in behind it, expecting the BMW to pass us both. Instead, it decelerated and ducked behind a different truck, disappearing from my view. That was strange. Stranger still was that I was watching cars in my rearview mirror and feeling paranoid. All this spy stuff was starting to get to me.

"Ta-ta," Charlie said into her phone. "Yes, me too."

She hung up and we drove in silence for a while.

"A friend of yours?" I asked.

"I'm not usually called by enemies."

"Boyfriend?"

She shook her head. "I don't date *boys*."

"You date girls?" I joked. "Not that there's anything wrong with that."

"He is a male friend. He's just not a boy."

"He must be special if you're going to bring in the New Year with him."

"He is special. We're going to be in Trafalgar Square, in the heart of London, with music and crowds and fireworks."

"That's not nearly as exciting as my plans."

She gave me a questioning look.

"I will be in a very exclusive location in downtown London in the company of a *rather* special lady."

"Is she an older woman?" Charlie asked.

"I'm too much of a gentleman to ever ask a lady her age, but I suspect she is a bit more sophisticated than I—a woman of the world."

Charlie reached over and gave my hand a squeeze. "There are far worse ways to spend the New Year than with my nana."

"I couldn't agree more."

"I really appreciate your being there with her. She's been so lonely since my grandfather passed on. They really were life partners. They set a very high bar. They had what I've always hoped I'll have one day."

I liked to think that if my father hadn't died, my parents would have had that sort of relationship too.

"She told me a lot about her husband, up there on the mountain. We joked about your grandfather and my grandpa being up in heaven together, looking down on us."

"That's sweet."

"So what does your grandmother think of your special man friend?" I asked.

"She doesn't really know him, although she definitely knows *of* him, if you know what I mean."

"You lost me at the second know."

"I hope that's the only thing that gets lost. There's our exit up ahead."

I took the exit. The BMW was right behind me.

EIGHT

I drove slowly through the campus, looking for the right building. It looked like a movie set—old ivy-covered brick and stone buildings, with long walkways cutting across manicured grounds. I was slightly distracted, though, and kept glancing in the rearview mirror, looking for the car that had followed me off the motorway. I'd pulled over and it had passed—glass tinted so dark I couldn't see inside—and then it was gone. I hadn't seen it since, but that hadn't stopped me from checking. Charlie had asked why I pulled over, and I'd said I wasn't sure about directions. No sense in sharing my paranoia.

I noticed we were getting more than our share of looks from the few students walking the campus. It was a pretty amazing car, and Charlie looked like the sort of person who belonged in a car like this. I felt like an imposter. I drank in the attention, pretending they both belonged to me. Not that a woman belonged to anybody—that was so wrong and sexist. I just mean I pretended I was her boyfriend... not that she dated boys. Whatever that meant.

"There's the building," she said.

There were open parking spots in front, so I pulled straight in, saved from having to try to parallel park from the wrong side of the car and road. Charlie was fiddling with her phone, texting. Probably to her friend.

"Are you coming or do you want to stay here?" I asked.

"Coming along."

We climbed out, and between the car and the girl, I felt a little bit like James Bond—or, at least, an actor playing James Bond. I sort of wished there were more people around to take it all in. If I was going to be in a movie, it should at least have a full house at the screening. I was sure that if Spencer were here, he would be telling me how the scene should be shot—maybe from above, from a helicopter.

It had been misting on the drive up and now it was starting to rain. I pulled my beret out of my pocket and slipped it on.

"A beret?" Charlie asked.

"Yes, a beret. Do you want to give me a hard time about it too?"

"'Too'? Let me guess. Charles made some snotty comment."

"Bingo."

"I told you, he's a git. Don't listen to anything he has to say." She walked over until she was standing only inches from me. She was much smaller than me, and she got on her tippy-toes, reached up and started to rearrange my beret. I felt a rush of heat, almost a flop sweat. This was stupid. I hardly even knew her, she had a *man* friend, we lived thousands of kilometers apart, we'd just met, and frankly, to be honest, she was way out of my league.

"Not many people can wear a beret," she said. She took a step back and studied me. I hoped I wasn't blushing too noticeably.

"Fortunately, you are one of those people. You definitely pull it off...nice look."

"It was my grandfather's...before he died."

"In that case, it is not only fashionable but wonderful, and you are sweet to honor his memory."

I couldn't hold her gaze any longer and looked down, now positive I was blushing. This was the second time she'd called me sweet. I wondered how her man friend would feel about her calling me that...although I knew it meant nothing. It was more like something you'd call a cute dog or an adorable toddler.

We started up the steps and tried to enter the building. The big door was locked. I tried a second door, with the same result, but a third opened. We stepped into a dark, empty corridor.

"It's a bit deserted with the Christmas break and all," Charlie said. "I'm surprised the professor is even on campus."

"He agreed to meet us here so we could see the diary. It's a book the Apostles keep that I need to look at." I pulled out a piece of paper. "His name is Dr. Moreau, and his office is room two thirty-four. The stairs are over here."

We started up. The stairwell was as dimly lit as the halls. I went to exit at the second floor and Charlie stopped me. "If it's two thirty-four, it's one floor higher, the second floor."

"But this *is* the second floor."

"We count them differently here. Two means two above the ground floor," she explained.

I couldn't even get climbing stairs right. We continued up to the next level and exited into the hallway. I started looking at the sequence of the rooms. At least I could still count. Up ahead, light was coming out of a slightly open door. It was room 234. I knocked and stuck my head in.

"Dr. Moreau?"

"Yes. You must be DJ."

"Yes, sir." We shook hands.

"And who is this?" he asked as Charlie entered the room.

"This is Charlie—Charlotte."

He took her hand and shook it, but this time he continued to hold on to her hand. He was staring at her in a way that made me feel uncomfortable. I wondered if Charlie had noticed as well.

"Yes, I'm Charlotte, and DJ is my *boyfriend*."

I startled. She pulled her hand away from him and took mine, which shocked me even more.

"Please, sit," Dr. Moreau said.

We settled into two seats across from him.

"Thank you so much for seeing us," I said, "especially on such short notice and during the holidays."

"I don't reside far from here. Besides, it was a special request from my dear friend Professor Higgins. How is Henry doing?"

"Very well," I said. What else could I say?

"He's a bit of an odd duck, but most geniuses tend to be that way," Dr. Moreau said. "I must admit that we don't get many requests concerning the Apostles." He paused. "And even if we did, we would never give out any information."

My heart dropped. Did this mean we'd come all this way for nothing?

"But as a favor, I will give you some relevant information. I was forwarded the names you were inquiring about, and I have *some* good news."

Which, of course, meant there was some bad news too. I was having a little trouble focusing on what he was saying with Charlie holding my hand.

Gently, I removed it. It was all sweaty, and I wiped it on my pants. She looked at me almost apologetically.

"We do, in fact, have two members with the name Johnson, one Hicks, and while we have no member with the last name Stanley, we did have a previous member who had the first name Stanley."

"And were either of the Johnsons members of the Apostles when Hicks or Stanley was there?" I asked.

"Sorry, but there was no overlap, and no Homer—either first or last name—and no Liszt."

"And I wouldn't imagine there would be a Birdie," I said.

"No Birdie, although there are a number of bird-like last names, including Peacock, Sparrow, Hawke and Finch. I actually knew Peacock...nice man, but rather long-winded sometimes and—"

"Finch?" I said, cutting him off. I thought of the name on the passport—Nigel Finch. "What if these names I gave you aren't surnames or even first names, but nicknames?"

"Birdie would certainly be an appropriate nickname for somebody named Finch or Hawke, I would imagine."

"What if they were all nicknames?" I asked.

"If they were, I'd have no way of knowing," Dr. Moreau said. "The book only lists the real names. I think you might have run into a blank wall."

"They're not nicknames," Charlie said. "They're cryptonyms."

"What?"

"Cryptonyms are code names given to spies, agents or operatives. The names you mentioned—Stanley, Homer, Hicks, Johnson and Liszt—are cryptonyms for five enemy agents."

"How do you know that?" I asked.

"I just googled the names." She held up her phone. "Their real names are Kim Philby, Donald Maclean, Guy Burgess, Anthony Blunt, and John Cairncross. They are collectively known as the Cambridge Five."

"Oh my goodness," Dr. Moreau said.

"Do you know these people?" I asked.

"I know *of* them. They are the greatest blight on the history of the Apostles club if not the whole history of Cambridge itself."

"It says here that they were all members of the club and were recruited by Russian agents to gather sensitive information about matters of national security and report it to the Soviets," Charlie said.

"They were all traitors," Dr. Moreau said, "and to our great shame they were all graduates of Cambridge and Apostles."

"But you said there were five, and I have six names," I said. "What about the sixth name, Birdie?"

"I'll read this to you," Charlie said, looking at her phone. "'While it was confirmed that there were five members of the sleeper cell, it—'"

"Did you say sleeper cell?" I said, cutting her off.

She nodded. I thought about the word *amoeba*—a cell—and then the five *z*'s above five of the six stick figures...a sleeper cell. That had to be what this was all about. There were too many coincidences for it not to be.

"Sleeper cells are groups of enemy agents planted in a country who perhaps don't take action for years or even decades while they undertake to infiltrate the highest levels of that government. Then, when nobody suspects, they gather secret information to report back to their masters," Dr. Moreau explained.

Charlie read, "'While it was confirmed that there were five members of the sleeper cell, it was widely believed that it included other members. Mentioned as possible other members of the sleeper cell were Michael Straight, Victor Rothschild and Guy Liddell.'"

But no Nigel Finch. And even if he was a spy, that didn't mean it was my grandfather. He never even went to Cambridge. Or did he? It felt like my head was spinning. I needed to go and get some fresh air.

"Kim Philby was the ringleader who recruited the other members. He himself was originally recruited by the Russians during the Spanish Civil War," Dr. Moreau said.

My ears perked up. My grandfather had fought in that war, on the same side as the Russians against the Fascists. Is that when all this started? Had he known Philby? I knew Steve had our grandfather's journal from when he served in the war. Maybe he could put the pieces together and find out if Grandpa and Philby were ever in the same place at the same time.

"The Cambridge Five all became high-ranking employees of different branches of British government, including security and diplomacy. After they infiltrated the British government, they sent information to their Russian handlers," Dr. Moreau explained.

I stood up. "Thank you for all your help," I said. I really needed to get out of there. My head was spinning and my stomach was churning. The professor got to his feet, and we shook hands.

"I'm glad I could offer you something. I just wish it didn't have any connection to the darkest chapter of our book," he said, holding it up. "To think that we had traitors in our midst who turned against our nation and betrayed its secrets and its well-being. So sad."

"Yeah, traitors. Thanks."

I hurried out of the room. Charlie trailed behind me.

"DJ!"

I didn't answer or even turn to respond. I just hurried down the stairs. I needed to get outside and breathe some fresh air. As I pushed out through the door, Charlie grabbed my arm and turned me around.

"DJ, what's wrong? You look like you've seen a ghost."

"Worse than a ghost. My grandfather could have been a traitor," I stammered.

"What are you talking about?"

"He had a passport that said his name was Nigel Finch. What if that was the Finch in the Apostles club? What if he was Birdie? What if he was in one of the sleeper cells and was giving secrets to the enemy? What if—?"

"That's *far* too many what ifs. There really is no proof, is there?"

I shook my head.

"Then don't believe the worst. Let's investigate further before you jump to any conclusions. What's our next step?" Charlie asked.

"I don't know. Let's just go back to your grandmother's home. Maybe the Holmesians came up with more information. Or maybe once we give them what we've found, they can take it from there."

"Wait," Charlie said. She came up close to me. "Don't turn around."

As soon as she said that, I almost turned around instinctively—but didn't.

"This will sound silly," she said, "but I think we might have been followed."

"Do you see the black BMW?" I asked.

"I don't know anything about a BMW. I'm talking about that motorcycle. As you go to climb in the Jag, look behind you—it's peeking out from behind a building. Act nonchalant, casual. Don't let him see you looking at him."

She got in, and I circled around the front of the car so that I could look back as I walked to the door. At first I didn't see anything, and then I noticed it, half hidden behind a building—the front end of a powerful motorcycle, a driver wearing a dark visor. I climbed into the car.

"I saw it, but what makes you think he's following us?"

"I saw a bike just like that after we left my nana's and then again on the motorway."

"It could be three separate motorcycles," I suggested.

"Maybe. Why were you mentioning a BMW?"

"There was one on the motorway that followed us when I made lane changes and then took the same exit as us," I explained.

"That could have been coincidence too," she said.

"Could be. I guess there's only one way to find out with the motorcycle."

I started the car and pulled away from the curb. I'd gotten no more than a few car lengths when the motorcycle pulled out from behind the building and turned in our direction.

"It's pulled out," I said. "Maybe it *is* following us."

I turned a corner and there was the black BMW with tinted windows, sitting at the side of the road. As I passed, it pulled out too.

NINE

I made a few more turns, just to see if we were being followed. The BMW and the motorcycle, which was behind it, would disappear with each turn and then reappear as I got farther along.

"Are they still with us?" Charlie asked. She was looking straight ahead, so as not to tip anyone off that we knew we were being followed.

"So what should I do?" I asked.

"Well, this *is* a Jag," she said. "Maybe you should try to lose them."

"Seriously. This isn't a movie. I have a better idea. I'm going to pull over and ask them what they want."

"You can't do that!" Charlie exclaimed.

"Why not?" I demanded.

"We have no idea who they are. Maybe they're car thieves trying to steal Nana's Jag. This is a very expensive car."

"So what do you think we should do?"

"Well, as I said, this is a Jag."

"I'm not going to go racing through the streets of Cambridge and get the two of us killed, me arrested or the car destroyed...but I will do a little something."

There was a red light up ahead, and traffic was settling in at the intersection. I slowed down and signaled for a left turn as I came up to the traffic. Already, vehicles were starting to fill in behind me. The BMW was now hidden behind a big truck, and the motorcycle must have been even farther back, as I couldn't see it anymore.

I saw a big gap in the oncoming traffic, so I gunned the engine and pulled out. There were cars coming, but I could get to the intersection before they did. I then hung a quick right turn, tires squealing. Rather than slowing, I pushed down on the accelerator and put some distance between us and our pursuers.

I glanced quickly in the rearview mirror—there was nothing behind us—and then hung another quick left to get out of sight and continue to race away.

"That was a rather clever move," Charlie said.

"Well, it *is* a Jag."

"Hang a left up ahead and that will take us over to the motorway."

There was still nobody in my rearview as I took the turn. "I just don't know why anybody would be following us."

"I have an idea...but I'm almost embarrassed to mention it," she said.

"Don't be embarrassed, just tell me."

"Paparazzi."

"Aren't those the guys who take pictures of celebrities?"

"Yes."

"Then why would they be following us—wait... they're following you! You think they want to take pictures of *you*?"

She shrugged and smiled. She really did look embarrassed. "This modeling thing has sort of started to take off...that and being around certain people."

"So how long has this been going on?" I asked.

"It hasn't been an issue yet, but I was warned it was probably going to start."

I laughed before I could stop myself, and she looked even more embarrassed. "I'm sorry. It's just that if I'd known that was a possibility, I wouldn't have done a James Bond move. I would have pulled over and let them take your picture."

"And your picture. They would have wanted to snap pictures of whoever I'm with, and right now I just can't have my picture taken with you."

"Sorry if I'm an embarrassment."

"It's not that. It's complicated, and I really can't explain it," she said. "Besides, why did *you* think we were being followed?"

I wasn't about to explain my paranoia, so all I said was, "I noticed the BMW was behind me and I thought it was weird."

"So you had *no* reason at all. At least my thoughts were grounded in some reality."

We drove along in silence. At least I had the rear-view mirror to attend to. So far, no black BMWs or motorcycles appeared in it.

"Nana's always talking about climbing Kilimanjaro with you," she said, breaking the silence with a safe topic.

"Your nana's pretty cool."

"I think so too."

"Kilimanjaro has an ongoing effect. I don't think there's one day that's gone by since I got down that it hasn't been in my thoughts," I said.

"I can imagine. And the pictures were so stunning."

"The pictures don't begin to capture it," I said. "It's something you have to experience."

"I'd love to do that. Are you going back?"

"Are you asking me to climb Kilimanjaro with you?" I joked.

"Nana has talked about returning one day—not to climb, mind you, but bringing me along. I think there might be space for a third person."

"I'm not sure what your boyfriend—I'm sorry, your *man*-friend—would think about that."

"I am free to make my own decisions. Isn't that how you treat your girlfriend?"

"Is that your clever way of asking if I have a girlfriend?" I asked.

"Well, do you?" she asked.

"Nobody serious right now."

"I would imagine I owe you an explanation for taking your hand and telling that professor you were my boyfriend."

"That did confuse me."

"I just hate when men, particularly much older men, look at me *that* way. I don't know if you noticed."

"I noticed." I just hoped she wasn't including me in that group of men who looked at her wrong.

"It's easier if they assume I'm *taken*, especially by somebody who's big and strapping and looks like he could beat the snot out of them...like you."

"I guess I'll take that as a sort of compliment."

"The whole concept of being taken, owned or possessed by a man is just so ancient, pre-feminist, and it's chauvinist garbage to begin with!"

"Don't get angry with me, it wasn't me who used the word."

"I know. It's just that—" Charlie stopped talking as her phone rang.

I could tell by the tone of her voice when she answered that it was him again. I didn't even know his name and I didn't like him. I had no information to base that on and no right to feel anything, certainly not jealousy, but still I did.

"I'm *so* looking forward to it," she said.

There was something about her voice, all soft and breathy and so English-accented, that it was almost like a drug, relaxing and soothing and exciting all at once. Why didn't girls in my area sound like that? I knew we all had accents—I had an accent. Maybe people here found my accent as adorable as I found hers...no, probably not.

"Me too," she said. "See you then." She hung up.

"Did he ask if you were with nobody again?"

"You know I didn't mean it that way. I owe you an explanation," she said.

"You don't owe me anything."

"Well, I'll give it to you anyway. As I said, this is all rather complicated. My friend is well known, and his relationships are scrutinized by the public and the press."

"Anybody who has so many relationships that they need to be scrutinized seems like trouble to me," I commented.

"It isn't the quantity but the *quality*. People wonder if the person he's seeing is good enough for him."

"If anybody has any question about you being good enough for him, they obviously don't know you."

"That is such a kind thing to say," she said. She offered another one of those wonderful smiles, and I felt my feet sort of melt.

It *was* kind, and although I meant it, I was surprised that I'd blurted it out.

"But to be honest, I've been wondering myself if I'm up to such standards," she said.

"His standards or somebody else's standards?"

"Mostly others'," she said.

"Mostly? If he isn't sure you're good enough for him, then he's a bigger git than your cousin. So he's famous...and rich?"

"Very rich and very famous."

"And hounded by paparazzi?"

"Everywhere he goes."

"So is that going to be a problem for your date on New Year's Eve?"

"Not a problem, but a solution. That's our official coming-out party. After that, everybody will know we're dating."

"Then I guess congratulations are in order," I said. This time I didn't mean it, or at least didn't feel it.

"Thank you."

I changed lanes again and watched in my rear-view as the car three back from us shadowed my moves—again. It wasn't a BMW or even black, but it did seem to be following us. A third tail or more coincidence? I wasn't even going to mention it.

"Could I see those papers again?" Charlie asked.

"Of course."

"I'm being careful. I wouldn't want to tickle us off into a ditch." Once again she reached into my jacket pocket, and once I again I flushed in response. She removed the papers, unfolded the sheets and began studying them.

"There's something about these numbers that's been troubling me," she said.

"The whole thing is just getting more troubling and more confusing. It seems like the more I find out, the less I know."

"But the numbers...something is so familiar about them. There must be a pattern of some sort that twigs a solution."

"The only pattern I can see is that while each of them is broken into different combinations, each line is ten numbers long," I said.

"Like a phone number."

"It can't be that simple...can it?"

"I know one way to find out for certain."

She pulled out her phone, put it on speaker so I could listen, and began dialing. With the first number, a recorded mechanical voice came on: "We're sorry; your call cannot be completed as dialed. Please check the number and dial again. This is a recording."

"So much for that theory."

"Lots of numbers are disconnected," Charlie said.

She tried the second and then the third number, with the same result—or lack of result.

"I still think there's something here if only I could..." She started laughing. "So simple and so silly."

She began dialing again. I expected the same recording to come on, but it didn't. This time, she got a ring.

"They were backward!" she exclaimed. "I recognized the area code for London as the last two digits on two of the numbers and—"

"Hello," a voice said on the other end of the phone. "Hello?" The voice was male, with an English accent, and he sounded older.

"Say something," Charlie mouthed. "Talk."

"Um...hello," I said. "This is...this is David McLean calling."

"David!" he exclaimed. "You shouldn't be calling on this line."

There was a click and then a dial tone.

"Should I redial?" Charlie asked.

I hesitated, thinking it through. "No. I don't know who he is, but I want to talk to him face to face."

"But you don't know where he lives, or even *who* he is," Charlie said.

"I think we can figure that one out. Right now, let's just get back to your nana's house."

I put on the turn signal and took the exit ramp.

"This isn't the exit!" Charlie exclaimed.

"Oh...sorry."

I slowed down, came to a stop and did a quick turn onto the entrance to the motorway. The white car had followed us off the highway, but it kept going and didn't follow us back on again. I was glad I hadn't mentioned it.

TEN

It felt good to tuck the Jag back into the garage, undented. As I swung the garage door closed and the car disappeared, I felt a rush of relief and a twinge of sadness. That was probably the last time I'd ever drive a Jag. I had kept both eyes on the road and glanced often in the rearview mirror and was so pleased that nobody—not motorcycles, BMWs, white cars or even trucks—had followed us home.

Doris greeted us as we entered the house, moving toward us on her crutches. "I have news! I have news about the meaning of the words!" Her expression grew more serious. "Although you might find it troubling...maybe we should sit down."

This couldn't be good. She motioned for us to sit, and she hobbled over and took a seat on one of the small settees.

"The Holmesians did a major search," she began, "and then got confirmation from other sources. It does seem as if your grandfather was possibly involved in the espionage game...in a most unsavory way. I'm afraid those names—Homer, Hicks and the others—well, they are what are called cryptonyms, or code names for agents, for five notorious traitors."

"The Cambridge Five," I said.

"Yes!" she exclaimed, sounding shocked. "But how did you find out? Was it that Dr. Moreau fellow?"

"He knew, but he's not the one who found out," I said. "That was all Charlie. She discovered it."

"But how?" Doris asked.

Charlie held up her phone. "I did a Google search. I put in the five names and it gave me a hit—actually, lots of hits."

"And that provided information?" Doris asked.

"Pages and pages. Everything we needed to know," I said.

"It's strange, but with the Internet, I guess anybody can find almost anything. I wonder what Sherlock Holmes would have done if he had had that tool at his fingertips," she said.

"Probably been even more amazing," I said. "And now we need the Internet again. I have to find a reverse directory."

"What is that?" Doris asked.

"If you have a phone number, you can plug it in and get the address and name of the person who has that number," I explained. I turned to Charlie. "Do you want to help me with that?"

"I'd like to...but..."

"You have someplace you have to be," I said—or, more to the point, she had to be someplace with some*body*.

"Yes. How about if you get the address and run through all those other numbers, and we'll start off first thing in the morning?" Charlie asked.

"That sounds like a plan," I agreed. "I'll stay here and spend a wonderful evening with somebody who definitely meets my standards...your nana."

Charlie looked hurt. I felt instantly guilty and wrong, but I didn't know what to say. I looked down at my feet. I hadn't meant to hurt her...although I was feeling hurt myself. There was no logic to it, but these things hardly ever have logic to them.

"You have a key to the house and of course you have my address," Doris said as I got ready to leave after an early dinner.

"Right here in my pocket," I said, patting it. "Along with my wallet, passport, camera, phone and directions. I'll be fine...but really, I should just stay in with you."

"You will *not* be spending your evening watching the telly with some old woman when you should be exploring London!"

"I won't be that late."

"And you'd better not be too early either," she said. "If you try to come in too soon, I'll put the chain on the door. You're young! Go out and meet some people; enjoy yourself." She paused. "I'm just so sorry that Charlie wasn't able to be here this evening to take you out."

"It's all right. She has a life, and I'm a big enough inconvenience as it is."

"Don't think of yourself that way, ever!" She pulled me to her and gave me a hug and a kiss on the cheek. "There's an umbrella at the front door. Try to stay dry, and enjoy yourself."

I grabbed an umbrella from the stand behind the door and headed off. It wasn't raining outside, but the air was cool and damp, and it looked like it could rain at any time. There were people on the street—a man walking his dog, a couple hand in hand, a businessman in suit and tie, a bowler hat on his head. Only in England. I had the directions to the river and the center of the city in my head and started to walk.

Doris's row house—which is what she called it—was no more than half a dozen streets from the Thames. From there, I was going to take a walking path along one side of the river into the center of the city, right by Parliament. I had hoped the walk would do me some good and clear my head, but my brain remained stuffed with thoughts and ideas.

I'd called all the numbers. None of them had come to anything. They were disconnected, reassigned—*it's been ours for fifteen years*—or they just rang and rang. I'd had the urge to call back the one number that had worked, to introduce myself again and see if there was more going on than an old man hanging up on somebody he didn't know.

Instead, I'd entered the phone number into a reverse directory and got an address—4030 Coventry Lane—and a name—B. March. Using my phone's GPS, I'd discovered that it was on the other side of London. If it had been closer, I would have walked over to scope it out that night.

I stopped at the intersection. There on the curb, in big letters, were the words *LOOK RIGHT!* Only in London were there crossing instructions for dummies. I did a quick look to the left before really looking to the right. There was nothing coming. I started to cross, and a black BMW with tinted windows rolled by. I startled slightly, thrown by its appearance. It kept going and disappeared at the next corner, hanging a right-hand turn. Big deal—the world is full of black BMWs, I told myself.

At each crossing, I looked to the right not just for traffic, but for motorcycles, black BMWs and white cars in particular. It was easy enough to see at least one of those on each street. I also became more aware of the people around me. Hadn't that woman been behind me for the last few blocks? And that man with the dog...I didn't recognize him, but that dog certainly looked familiar. This was becoming ridiculous. *I* was becoming ridiculous. At least Charlie had a reason to think she was being followed.

The river loomed up ahead. I could smell it, a scent even stronger than the faint dampness in the air itself. The wind was blowing down the river and I could feel it through my jacket. I pulled up my collar and fought the urge to turn around and go back to Doris's house, remembering she had said she wasn't going to let me in if I came back too early. It wasn't cold like back home, but there was a rawness that made it seem colder than it was. At least the rain was still holding off.

I turned my back to the wind and pulled out my phone. This was probably a good time to text Steve.

`I need you to look in Grandpa's war journal for any references to a man named Kim Philby. He could also be called Stanley. Let me know asap. This is important. Thanks. Hope all is good.`

I pushed *Send*. Now I'd just have to wait for his answer.

The path I was standing on was wide and well traveled by joggers and cyclists and people pushing baby carriages. I passed by more than one couple around my age walking hand in hand. I fantasized about seeing Charlie walking hand and hand with her man friend and played around with what I'd say to her—or him. I wondered if I'd know who he was. Was she dating some musician or movie star? That was probably as far-fetched as my thinking I was being followed.

Anyway, she wasn't going anywhere public with this mystery man. How special did he think he was that he had any doubts about being seen in public with her? What did that even mean? Was he a celebrity, or was it something else? Was he married? Was that it? I felt terrible even thinking that. I figured Charlie was better than that.

"Excuse me," a woman called out. She had a heavy foreign accent. I stopped. "Do you think you could take a picture of my husband and me?"

"Oh, of course."

"It is a very tricky camera," the man said. His accent was also very thick...something Eastern European. "First you stand with my wife and I will take picture... set it up...then you take our picture."

"Yeah, I guess I—"

She grabbed me by the arm and, with remarkable strength, pulled me forward and to the side.

"Say smiley!" he called out. I gave a weak smile and the flash went off. Then it went off a second and third time.

"Now you take us picture...come, George," she called out to her husband.

He handed me the camera, and then he and his wife posed. I positioned myself so that I could frame them in one side of the picture with the London Eye visible behind them.

"Okay, smile," I said.

I took one picture and then a second to be safe. "I think I got a good one."

"Thank you so much," he said as he took back the camera.

"Yes, thank you. People here are so friendly. What is your name, so I can put it down in my trip memory book?"

"It's...um...Nigel. Nigel Finch." I don't know why I told her that, but I did. It popped out without thinking.

"Good to meet you. If you gave your email, we could send you a copy of picture if you'd like," he said.

"That's all right, but thank you just the same. Have a good evening."

I started off again. It was good to talk to somebody, yet somehow it made me feel even more alone. Everybody walking along here seemed to have somebody except me. I was by myself—whoever that self was. Why had I said *Nigel Finch* when I'd been asked my name? Was it because I didn't want them to know anything about me, or was it because I was trying out another name? What if we found out my grandfather really wasn't David McLean? Would we take on the family name Finch? I certainly couldn't see myself as a Nigel. It was still strange enough to be called David instead of DJ. For years I'd just been DJ—David Junior—named after my grandfather. It was after his death—in the letter he'd written me—that he said I could be called David now.

I looked up and saw the Parliament buildings looming in front of me. I wasn't any less alone, but I felt a surge of excitement. It all came back in a rush. Here I was, standing beside the Thames River, in London, England, beside the very seat of modern democracy. This was all pretty darn cool. But maybe my grandfather had worked to try to bring about the downfall of democracy—that wasn't so cool. I had to stop thinking like that.

Just downriver and on the other side, the London Eye rotated slowly, a gigantic Ferris wheel rising above the river. It glowed red and white in the darkening sky. I'd read that it was 135 meters high. I don't like planes, but I don't mind heights—well, not as much. From up there, I was sure, I could see the entire city.

I crossed over the bridge to the other side of the river. I bought a ticket and joined the line for the Eye. Looking up, I counted the cars—thirty-two—each an enclosed glass container that held a couple dozen passengers.

"Pretty amazing, isn't it?" a man asked me.

"Yeah, it is."

"You're Canadian," he said.

"Yeah, I am...how did you know?"

"The accent."

I hadn't said more than a few words. Was it that obvious?

"It's easy for me to tell because I'm a Canuck too."

He didn't sound Canadian. "Really?"

"Well, I guess it gets a little blurred because I lived in New York for a long time, eh?"

"Yeah, that could be it. You do sound more like an American."

"And we Canucks don't want to be mistaken for American, right?"

I shrugged. "I like Americans. It's no big deal." Unless a beautiful girl didn't know the difference.

We continued to shuffle forward in the line.

"We're moving pretty quick, eh?" he said.

This was one really friendly guy, and he was making me super uncomfortable.

We got close to the front of the line. A big capsule stopped and the glass doors slid open. The attendant herded a group of people in. I hoped I'd get in this one—and that my friend wouldn't. I got on, but he got on with me. One out of two wishes granted.

While others flocked toward the glass sides, I took a seat in the middle of the compartment, on a circular bench. I felt more comfortable with a little distance between me and the sides. As others crowded in, I had a wall of people as protection.

"You nervous around heights too?" a familiar voice asked. Before I could answer, my "friend" said, "Maybe it's a Canuck thing, eh?"

I'd never heard anybody use "Canuck" so often... or say "eh" so much.

"Rob. Rob Davies," he said, offering his hand.

I hesitated for half a second. "Nigel Finch." At least I was consistent. Besides, I didn't want him to know my real name.

"Pleased to meet you, Nigel." He gave me a hearty handshake. "So what brings you to London, business or pleasure?"

"Visiting a friend."

"It's good to have friends. I make them everywhere I go. Speaking of which"—he tapped the shoulder of a man standing just in front of us—"can you take a picture of me and my new friend Nigel?"

He handed the man the camera and then crowded in close to me, throwing an arm around my shoulder. Before I could react, the man was taking a picture, and then another. Captain Canuck released his grip on me as he took back his camera. I took the opportunity to escape.

"I want to get a better view," I explained as I got to my feet and walked away from him.

Everybody always talked about big cities being unfriendly. I might have to start visiting bigger cities.

ELEVEN

DECEMBER 30

I pulled up the garage door and the Jag smiled at me with its big chrome grill. I smiled back. It was going to be wonderful to drive it one more time. I stepped inside and ran my hand along the hood. "Hello, my darling," I said.

Charlie grabbed the door and swung it down, sealing us inside. I gave her a questioning look.

"I thought the two of you might want to be alone."

"Then shouldn't you be outside the door?" I asked.

"I am leaving, and you're coming with me." She took me by the hand, and an instant rush of heat surged through my body. She led me through the little side door and out into a small alley beside the garage.

"What are we doing?" I asked.

"We're not taking the Jag," she said, leading me down the alley.

"Why not?"

"I was followed here today by two men on motorcycles...paparazzi."

I skidded to a stop. "So you think somebody might take your picture, and I might be in it. That's why I can't take the Jag?"

She looked embarrassed.

"So what are we going to do instead—walk across the city?"

"I was thinking a cab or the underground. Those are both genuine English experiences."

"As is driving a Jag," I said.

"*Please.* I'll even pay for the alternate transportation."

She looked at me with big blue, pleading eyes. She was using me against myself in this argument. And I was losing. "Okay. Let's go."

She dragged me, still holding my hand, between the garages, through a little gate and then over a small fence that we just stepped over. We came up to the side of another house. She peeked out and then retreated back behind the house. She released my hand—my very sweaty hand—and pulled something out of her bag.

"Put this on," she said, handing me a baseball cap.

"Gee, and I didn't get you anything."

"Just put it on. It's a disguise."

I removed my beret, carefully folded it and put it in my pocket, replacing it with the cap. She pulled out a brown wig, put it on and tucked all her hair underneath it. Next, she put on a big floppy hat.

"How does that look?" she asked.

"It looks like you're more paranoid than you think I am. What now?"

"I'm going to walk down to the main intersection, and you're going to wait for a minute or two and then follow. Hopefully, by the time you get there I will have hailed a cab, and we'll be off."

"Should we synchronize our watches?" I asked. "Or maybe we should have a password if we suspect danger. How about I say 'Tower of London'? Would that work?"

"I don't have a watch, but you can say anything you want. You know, you really do wear that beret better than the baseball cap. See you in a minute."

She trotted off, and I stood there watching. I wanted to drive that Jag, but I wanted to be with her more. I looked at my watch. It had been long enough. I ran after her. She had already climbed into a big black cab, leaving the door open. I jumped in after her and closed the door behind me.

"Okay, let's go," she said to the driver. She was slumped down in the seat, with only the top of her head—the part covered by the hat and wig—showing.

"The address is—"

"Just drive for a while," Charlie said, cutting me off. "I want to show my friend a little bit of London. Head toward the East End."

Without being asked, I slumped down in my seat as well. It was a big old cab, the sort you see in movies set in London. As we started to travel, I inched up in my seat. If I wasn't going to drive, at least I could take advantage of being a passenger. Coincidentally, we headed along a route almost identical to the one I'd walked the previous night. The Houses of Parliament were on one side, the Eye on the other. Despite its height, and the pushy "Canuck," I'd enjoyed the Eye—the ride and the view. It was a beautiful city.

After this little adventure came to its inevitable dead end, I'd have a couple of days to enjoy the sights before I headed back. I might even take in New Year's Eve in Trafalgar Square. I wouldn't be with Charlie, of course, but it was a free country, and I could still enjoy the evening with thousands and thousands of other people.

"You can give him the address now," Charlie said.

"To 4030 Coventry Lane, please."

"Oh, that's a classy part of town. Very old-money," the cabdriver said.

"Could you drive by the house first, please?" Charlie asked when we got to Coventry Lane.

That sounded like a good idea. I'd felt increasingly nervous as we got closer. What exactly was I supposed to say? I eyed the house, which was similar to all the homes along this street. It was large, brick, partially covered by ivy, set back from the road by a lawn and marked off by a stone wall. One difference was that 4030 had a higher wall than the others and a grated metal gate.

"Pull over here, please, just around this corner."

The driver pulled into a narrow alley, and the house was lost from view behind another house's perimeter wall.

"Here's the fare and another fiver," Charlie said, passing the money over the seat. "I want you to wait five minutes or so. We might be right back."

"Sure thing," the driver replied.

This was the first time I'd noticed the driver; his accent made it obvious he wasn't English.

We got out, and I started toward the front of the house. But Charlie headed down the lane, and I went after her. She pulled off her hat and wig, and I pulled off my baseball cap as well. She stuffed everything into her big purse.

"I thought we'd walk around the grounds first, just to have a look," she explained.

That made sense. Anything to delay having to knock on the front door made sense. What was I going to say? *Hello, I'm David McLean. Do you know my grandfather? And by the way, was he a spy or a traitor or a sleeper agent?* Yeah, that was a good opening line.

The wall surrounding the property was slightly taller than me, so while I could see the house, I couldn't see the yard at all. When we passed by a metal gate, we saw an old man puttering in the garden. We stopped.

"Hello!" Charlie called out.

He looked up from his work, peered around in a confused manner and then saw us. He waved back, smiled and gave a little tip of his hat. Still holding the shovel, he slowly limped toward us. As he got closer, I saw that he was of my grandfather's vintage. He could have known him.

"Good morning. Your garden looks lovely," Charlie said.

"Thank you very much."

"And this is your house?" she asked.

"I hope so, or I'm tending somebody else's garden... although I'm afraid this spring weather has been so unpredictable that it's made for a bit of a hodgepodge."

He must have meant spring*like*; compared to home, this was spring. It certainly wasn't like the winter where I came from.

"I'm Charlie and this is my friend DJ."

"I'm Bernard," he said.

"I'm afraid my mother would be very angry at me for addressing somebody who is my elder by their first name," Charlie said.

"Your mother is obviously a person of breeding. My name is Mr. March."

He reached out through the grating, and we each shook his hand.

"Pleased to make your acquaintance, Mr. March, sir," I said.

"We're just out for a stroll. Would you like to join us?" Charlie asked.

"I have so much work to do, but it would be nice," he said.

I went to open the gate, but it wouldn't budge.

"Locked," he said, "but I do believe I have the key right here." He searched his pockets and finally produced a full ring of keys. His hand was shaking.

"Besides, it would give me a chance to see how much damage was done last night," he said as he fumbled with the keys, trying to find the right one.

"Damage?" I asked.

"From the bombers. They must have been close, because it felt as if they were going to shake me out of my bed."

Charlie and I exchanged confused looks.

"I hope there weren't too many casualties. It's hard enough when soldiers are killed in war, but the Blitz targets civilians. Terrible."

"But the Blitz—" I began.

"Is a terrible thing, a tragedy," Charlie said. "But there were only a few bombers last night, and they dropped their bombs wide of any target. There's not much to see."

"There's not anything to see," I said to her.

"Well, there might be something to hear," Charlie said as an aside. "I bet Mr. March has many stories he could tell us. Right, sir?"

"Oh, so many stories to tell and…" There was a click, and the gate opened slightly.

I moved in close to Charlie so I could speak quietly to her. "Look, there really isn't a point in doing this…he's obviously senile…what is he really going to be able to tell us?"

"You'll never know until you find out."

There was no way to argue *that* logic. I pulled my beret out and put it on my head.

"David?" Mr. March said.

"Yes," I said.

His eyes were wide open. And then I remembered that Charlie had introduced me as DJ. He was looking at me but seeing my grandpa.

"You shouldn't have come here," he said. "What if somebody is watching? This could destroy years of effort, blow your cover and—"

"Hey, what are you doing?" a voice yelled.

I looked past Mr. March. Coming out of the house was a large man in a suit and tie.

"Stop right there!" he yelled as he ran toward us. He looked angry.

"Go!" Mr. March yelled. "Get away, and I'll hold him off!" He tossed the keys to me and I caught them. He slammed the gate shut with a loud thud.

"But, but—"

"Come on!" Charlie yelled. She grabbed me by the hand and dragged me away, and then we both started to run.

"We have to get away," she yelled.

We raced down the alley and made the turn. Thank goodness the cab was still waiting. We jumped in, and Charlie yelled at the driver to take off. He squealed away before I'd even settled in, and I was practically flung on top of Charlie. I struggled to disentangle myself without putting my hands anywhere I shouldn't, then looked out the back window at the receding view of the wall and the house. We'd gotten away; we were safe. And then a big white car—a Mercedes—turned onto the street behind us.

TWELVE

Charlie turned around so she could see the vehicle too. It was following at a discreet distance, not gaining but staying with us.

"Could be coincidence," I said.

"Driver, could you please make a series of random turns?" Charlie said.

"You want me to lose him instead?" he asked. "I noticed car as well. Do you think the two cars are working together?"

"Two cars?" I repeated.

"White Mercedes was on our tail on drive out and waited down the street, and then black BMW started in."

I looked back, beyond the Mercedes, and there was a BMW.

"If we had an elephant or two, we'd have ourselves a parade, we would," the driver said.

He made a quick turn, and I was flung from one side of the cab to the other, hitting against the door.

"You should have seat belt," he said.

I fumbled around, but no luck. "I can't find the seat belt!"

"There is no seat belt."

"But you told me I should have a seat belt!" I protested.

"You should, but I no have. Most unfortunate."

Charlie was still peering out the back window. "You need to lose them."

"They are BMW and Mercedes. I am bucket of bolts without even seat belts, but I will try."

He made another quick left turn, but this time I was ready.

"Who are these people in car?" he asked. "Are they police?"

"Not police, but we're not sure who they are. We want to lose them," I explained.

"How bad you want to lose them?" the driver asked.

"Really bad."

"I can do, but it will cost...oh...maybe fifty pounds," he said.

"How will money make this car go faster?" I demanded.

"Not faster, but will have help. Is it worth?" he asked.

"Yeah, do it."

"First money," he said. "Let me see money."

I pulled out my wallet. I had over a thousand pounds in there and quickly pulled out the cash he wanted. I went to hand it to him, but Charlie stopped me.

"You can see the money," she said to the driver. "We need to see the results before you get it."

He grabbed the radio and started talking. I didn't know the language, yet it sounded familiar. Was it Polish or Russian? Definitely it was something Eastern European. He barked out words, and replies came back over the radio from at least three different voices, all speaking the same language.

"We cannot outrun but we can hide. I have arranged. Now tell me why these people follow but not wish to catch."

"How do you know they don't want to catch us?" I asked.

"They are in Mercedes and BMW and we are in bucket of bolts. If they wish to catch, they would have caught."

That made perfect sense. What was the point in following us if they weren't going to overtake us? Were they back there waiting to take a picture? Was that what it was?

He turned onto a broad, busy street with every lane full. It seemed like every second vehicle on the road was a cab, and a lot of them looked identical to ours. Our driver continued to yell things into the microphone, and equally excited responses came back.

"Here is help," our driver said.

I looked through the windshield. All I saw was a bunch of cabs. Wait, was that what we were doing, hiding in plain sight? We passed between two cabs, and the drivers waved. Then another cab came into the gap behind us. I turned and looked through the back window. The three cabs were now side by side, and we quickly left them behind as we sped up and they slowed down. Then all three of them suddenly came to a stop. They were forming a roadblock, filling all the lanes! I could hear car horns sounding as we took off.

"That was brilliant!" Charlie exclaimed.

"Not brilliant. Just teamwork. I split the money with my friends in other cabs." He reached a hand over the back of the seat and rubbed his thumb against his fingers. I handed him the fifty pounds. "So where I drive now?"

"I guess we should head back to your grandmother's," I said.

"No, I think that's the last place we should go. That has to be where they'll head to try to locate us again." She leaned over the seat. "I need an Internet café, someplace crowded where we can disappear."

"I know such a place," the driver said.

"Aren't you afraid of having your picture taken with me in public?" I asked.

"In public isn't so much a problem. There needs to be a crowd."

"This place is so crowded it is like clown car in Moscow Circus," the driver said.

"Here is place," the driver said.

I pulled out my wallet and gave him the amount of money on the meter plus a tip. It was easy to be generous when I had this much money.

"Thanks for getting us away," Charlie said.

"Thank you for money."

We went to get out, and he stopped us. "Wait, wait, you will need cab again. You should call me and I will come."

"Thanks for the offer, but we don't want to put you to any bother," Charlie said.

"No bother. You pay me money. You may need driver who can get you out of problems again, and for me, that was most fun time. Here, take my number. This way you no need to stand around where you can be seen on road." He handed Charlie a business card.

She looked at it. "Thank you, *Jack*."

"Not real name, but what I get called now. I am in England, need to have name like English. When I am in London, I am Jack."

"We'll call in an hour or so," Charlie said. "If you're around, that would be wonderful."

"I will be around."

We climbed out onto the crowded sidewalk, and he drove away. It was reassuring to know he was only a call away. With everything going on, it felt good to have somebody else—and his friends—on our side.

I followed Charlie into a crowded building. The sign indicated it was a combination cafeteria, laundromat and Internet café. I didn't need anything washed, but I certainly was hungry—and curious. I hoped I'd have those two desires satisfied. We moved through the crowded main floor, where not a table, washing machine or computer seemed to be available, and up the stairs to the next level. There we found a table, and while Charlie ordered for us, I logged into the computer.

"Well?" she asked.

I finished typing *Bernard March* into Google and hit *Enter*. "Just loading now...wow...look at all the entries."

"*Sir* Bernard March," Charlie said. "If that's the same person, he must have done something pretty important to be knighted by the Queen."

I looked at the pictures. They were all of a much younger man, although he certainly bore a resemblance to the person we'd met. I scanned down, looking for a birthday to confirm that this was the right Bernard before I wasted any more time on his profile. There it was. He was born seven years after my grandfather. That would make him about the age of the person we had just met. I went back up to the top of the page.

I started to read out loud. "*Sir Bernard March led a distinguished life in service to the British government during both World War Two and the Cold War. He worked first as a cryptographer, then in intelligence analysis, ultimately rising within first MI5 and subsequently MI6*. What's MI6?" I asked.

"It's the British equivalent of the American CIA. We call it the SIS—Secret Intelligence Service."

"Okay. In Canada, it's CSIS—Canadian Security Intelligence Service."

"I thought you only had hockey players and lumberjacks in Canada," Charlie said.

"And I thought you only had crumpet eaters and members of the royal family here in England. Would you like me to go on with this?"

"Probably best that we continue. My apologies... I didn't know you Canadians were so sensitive."

I ignored her. "*Due to the secretive nature of the organization, and for reasons of national security, there are significant gaps in our information concerning both the outside life of Sir March and his specific assignments within that organization. However, it is widely believed that Sir March was the director or assistant director of MI6 for a period of no less than twenty-five years. As is customary with former directors, his whereabouts are currently unknown, but he is presumed to be alive and living in retreat somewhere in the United Kingdom.*"

"Alive and living at 4030 Coventry Lane in London," Charlie said.

I continued to read. "*Ian Fleming, the creator of fiction's most famous spy, James Bond, and a former member of the intelligence community, once noted that nobody in this country knows more about where the skeletons are buried than our own Sir Bernard 'Bunny' March—*"

I stopped and looked up at Charlie. "Bunny March...Haigha...the March Hare...he's the one in the notebook entry. Haigha knows. He's the one that knows the truth!"

"Maybe it's just a bizarre coincidence," she said.

"A coincidence that his phone number is on the list, that he knows my grandfather's name, that he's the one who knows where all the skeletons are buried?"

Charlie put one hand on my arm and made a calming gesture with the other. "You're attracting a little bit of attention...a little quieter, please...especially when you're talking about buried skeletons."

I looked around. There were a lot of people staring at us with questioning expressions. "Sorry, but it has to be him." Then I realized what that meant. "And that brings us to a dead end. He can't help me at all. Maybe he once knew a lot, but now he doesn't even know what year it is."

"Maybe he can still help," Charlie said.

"Help with what? He thinks it's spring and World War Two is still happening, that he was shaken out of bed last night by the Blitz."

"Again, a little more quietly, please," Charlie said. "My grandmother on my father's side suffered from Alzheimer's. It started slowly and she declined to the point where she hardly recognized my father at the end. But even then, she could still tell us vivid details about her childhood, about the war—things we knew were true."

"So you think that even if he doesn't know what season or year it is, he might know about my grandfather and his history?"

"He did remember the name. He did look at you and think you were your grandfather, so why not?" she asked. "Besides, what else have you got? Let me write down some of this information." She pulled a paper napkin out of the holder. "Do you have a pen?"

"I don't think so." I tapped my jacket pocket and felt something. I pulled out a pen—*where did that come from?*—and handed it to her.

"This is a *very* expensive pen," she said, holding it up. "Where did you get this?"

I shook my head. "I have no idea, but I think these are probably more important." I fished out the keys Sir Bunny had thrown to me.

"My goodness, you have the keys to the home of the former head of MI6!"

"Could you keep *your* voice down now?" I hissed. "I may only have the keys to the back gate."

"Well, that's at least a start when we go back to talk to him."

"I don't think that angry man who chased us away is going to invite us in to continue the conversation," I noted.

"He's probably an agent assigned to protect Sir March and make sure that he doesn't inadvertently give out information. What's in his head would be pretty valuable to the right people."

"So he's not going to let us ask him questions," I said.

"Leave him to me. Let's finish our meal and give Jack a call."

"Excuse me," a girl at the next table said. "I don't mean to interrupt you, but do you think I could have your autograph?" She had a magazine in her hands.

"Certainly," Charlie said.

As she took it, I looked at the cover. There was Charlie—an all-made-up, deluxe version of her—on the cover of British teen *Vogue* magazine. She used my pen to sign her name in a flurry and handed the girl back the magazine.

"And can I have a photo?" the girl asked.

"Of course."

The girl thrust her phone at me and then squatted beside Charlie. I snapped a picture and handed the phone back to the girl. She thanked Charlie profusely and practically danced away.

"You really are a celebrity," I said.

"Not what I'd like, but it'll pay my tuition. I guess we do what we have to do sometimes. Which means going back to talk to Sir Bunny."

Jack pulled the car into the lane down from Mr. March's house. It felt good to have a getaway car. We'd agreed that while Jack waited here, I would go to the back of the property and wait. Charlie was going to go to the front gate, ring and try to occupy the attendant—the agent. He probably had a gun; did he have a license to kill, like James Bond? We figured he was probably some low-level MI6 operative assigned to keep tabs on Mr. March, but he would still be carrying a weapon. If we had figured out that Mr. March had lots of information to give away, then we probably weren't alone in that thought.

I peeked through the gate and was surprised to see Mr. March—Sir March—still out puttering in the yard. It had been hours since we'd left, and he was still digging in what I thought was the same flower bed as when we'd first seen him.

My phone buzzed, and I looked at the message. It was from Charlie. It was one word—Now.

I called out. "Mr. March, sir."

He looked up at me, smiled and waved. He pushed the shovel into the ground and came over, moving very quickly.

"We haven't got much time," he said. He looked over his shoulder anxiously.

"I just have a few questions."

"Do you still have the keys?" he asked.

"Yes, I do." I was surprised he'd remembered. I pulled them out of my pocket, and he reached out and snatched them from my hands. He looked through the keys, found one and inserted it in the lock; it clicked, and the gate opened. He stepped out into the alley.

"I knew you'd come back and get me, David," he said. "I knew you wouldn't leave me a prisoner."

"Hey, come back!"

I looked past him. *Two* men were running out of the house! Sir March slammed the gate shut with a thud. "Let's get going!"

"But, but..."

"Where is your car?" he demanded.

"It's this way, but—"

"No time for arguing. Let's go!"

He started off, and I was unfrozen by the sound of the men practically slamming into the gate, screaming and straining to get it open. I started running, surprised at how far the old guy had gone. He was really moving! I grabbed his hand and steered him around the corner. Charlie was already standing there with the door open. Before I could say a word, Sir March climbed into the cab.

"Get in!" I screamed. Charlie jumped into the car, and I practically hurled myself in after her, landing in a heap. Jack threw the car into reverse, skidded out onto the street and then squealed away. I pulled myself upright and peered out the back window. Nothing came into view, and then Jack hit the next intersection, leaving everything behind.

"What did you do?" Charlie demanded.

"I was just trying to talk to him."

"Talk? You've kidnapped him!"

"Hardly," Sir March yelled. "You're a hero, David. I must get to the prime minister's home immediately! I have vital information that Winston must get!"

"Do you realize what we've done?" Charlie said. "You're going to have the police and half of British Security looking for us!"

Jack looked over his shoulder. "I have place where we can go and you can talk, where nobody will be looking for nobody."

"Get us there," Charlie ordered. "And quickly!"

Jack pulled the cab into an alley between two deserted buildings. He wasn't kidding: nobody was going to be looking for us here. I'd been watching out the rear-view the whole way, and I was positive nobody had followed us.

"This is perfect," I said. "Thank you."

"You need to get out of cab now," Jack said.

"We could just talk right here," Charlie said.

"No, you do not understand." Jack raised a gun above the seat. "You will get out right here."

THIRTEEN

"What are you doing?" I gasped.

"People with guns ask questions. People without guns do as they are told." He raised the gun and aimed it right at me. "Now!"

I suddenly realized we weren't alone. Another man, wearing a dark suit and darker sunglasses, was at the car door beside me. He was holding a pistol, and he looked vaguely familiar. He opened the door and motioned with the pistol for me to come. Slowly, with hands raised, I shuffled across the seat and out of the car, followed by Sir March and then Charlie.

"I—I don't understand," I stammered. "What's going on?"

"It's obvious, David. We've stumbled into a trap," Sir March said. "Our driver obviously is a double agent."

I looked at Jack.

"Not double agent, just agent," he said.

The two men led us into one of the buildings. It was almost empty except for some long-abandoned industrial equipment, dirty, broken down and dusty. They took us to a smaller room. Here, things were very different. It was like stepping from one universe to another. This well-lit room was filled with new furniture, and there was a computer sitting on a desk. On the wall behind the desk was a bank of TV monitors. They showed images from closed-circuit cameras set up on the outside of the building. In one, I saw our cab parked in the alley.

"Sit," Jack said, and the three of us sank into seats at one end of the room. The two men then went to the other end of the room and started talking in a foreign language.

"As I thought," Sir March whispered. "Russian... they must be KGB."

"Do you know what they're saying?" Charlie whispered back.

"My Russian isn't the best, but they seem to want some information. And I know they'll be prepared to do whatever is needed to get that information." He turned directly to me. "You'd know about that, though, wouldn't you, David?"

I had no idea what he was talking about, but I nodded my head in agreement. The two men stopped talking and came back to stand in front of us.

"Look, this is all some kind of mistake," I said.

"Is it a mistake, Mr. Nigel Finch?" the second man asked.

The voice. It all came back to me. "You're the man from by the river. I took your picture with your wife."

"She is not my wife."

"And that's not really my name," I said.

"We are aware of that," Jack said. "We know who Mr. Finch is, and we also know that your name is McLean. What we don't know is why you chose to use that name—Finch."

"And believe me, you will tell us," the second man said. "But first we will deal with the important things."

He went and stood directly over Sir March. "And are we to believe that you are not Bernard March?"

"You can believe whatever you want to believe," Sir March said. "I just want you to know that before we're finished here, you're going to regret the day you were born."

Jack snickered. "Empty words."

"We'll see how funny it is once Winston lets Stalin know how you've been treating your allies."

The two men turned to each other. They looked confused.

"He thinks it's the forties and the war is still on," I explained.

"We are aware. You! Get to your feet!" Jack grabbed Sir March and pulled him to his feet.

"Be careful—he's old," I said.

The other man pointed the gun directly at my head. "You be careful or you will not have a chance to become old."

Jack led the old man away, leaving the three of us in the room.

"Look," I said. "The girl has nothing to do with any of this. If you let her go, I'll tell you everything."

"You will tell us everything whether we let her go or not. She stays."

"Okay, but can you at least tell me what the name Nigel Finch means to you?"

He shrugged. "To me it means nothing. It is a waste of time and resources to be chasing a phantom."

"What do you mean, a phantom?"

"Maybe I don't use the word right. A ghost from the past."

"How far in the past?" I asked.

"Long before you were born and even before I was born," he said.

"Then how did you even know to come looking for me?" I asked.

"There was increased traffic on the Internet," he explained. "Many people started looking for certain significant names, obviously doing research."

It was the Holmesians. It had to be. "The Cambridge Five were Russian agents feeding information to your government. Finch was the sixth," I said.

"Go on."

I suddenly realized that I'd been trying to get information out of him when in fact he was getting information out of me.

"I don't know anything else. I just got caught up with these old geezers who belong to the Sherlock Holmes society thing. As far as I know, this Nigel Finch is just a character in a novel by Arthur Conan Doyle."

"Really? And is that why you went and kidnapped the former director of MI6?" He laughed. "By the way, we should thank you for saving us the trouble of doing it ourselves."

"You mean you were *planning* on kidnapping him?"

"His mind may be scrambled, but there are pieces up there"—he tapped his head—"that might be worth knowing. Kidnapping him makes sense, but you two are a waste of my time."

"Sorry to inconvenience you."

"You know somebody will realize we're missing and call the police," Charlie said.

"The police will not even take a missing-person report until the person has been missing for at least twenty-four hours. Even then, they will think it is two young people going off for a little fun around the holidays."

"My parents know I wouldn't do that," Charlie said.

"Then they can look. This is a big city, and we are very isolated here. Now I want silence."

I watched on the closed-circuit screens as day turned to night. Two others had come in and brought us all cold fish and chips. We'd been allowed to get up, stretch and go to the washroom, with a guard stationed outside the windowless toilet. Twice Jack had come back, but we hadn't seen Sir March.

I was afraid to think about what was happening to him and even more afraid of what it might lead to when it was my turn to be questioned. What exactly was I supposed to tell them when I didn't know anything? Well, anything except the fact that my grandfather might have been the Russian agent they were looking for. No, wait—if they were looking for him, that meant they didn't know where he'd gone or what had become of him. Maybe he wasn't a Russian agent but somebody who was tricking them into thinking he was a traitor. That would make him a triple agent instead of a double agent. Wouldn't that be better?

I looked up. On the desk by the screens were our phones, my wallet and Charlie's purse. If we could get to a phone without our guard seeing, maybe we could call the authorities and get the police here.

I thought I saw some movement on one of the screens. I looked harder but couldn't see anything. It must have been my eyes playing tricks on me, nothing more than wishful thinking. Then there was more movement—it was an old woman pushing a shopping cart full of what looked like cardboard and cans.

"She is always here," the man said. "Maybe she will break in and rescue you." He laughed. "You might as well go to sleep."

FOURTEEN

DECEMBER 31

Still mostly asleep, I tried to move my arm, but it seemed to be stuck. I pulled harder, and then I opened my eyes. Charlie was cuddled against me, pinning my arm under her head. I startled completely awake as I remembered everything. Across from us, his head down on the desk, sat one of our captors. He was asleep too. Maybe we could sneak out. Then I saw the gun on the desk beside him, not more than a foot away from his hand. There was no point in trying to run if all he had to do was wake up and shoot us as we left. I was fast, but not nearly as fast as a bullet.

"Charlie," I whispered. She didn't respond.

Slowly, carefully, I slid my arm out from under her head. She mumbled something, and then her eyes opened. I gestured for her to be quiet. I looked over. The man hadn't roused. I got to my feet, and the couch groaned ever so slightly. I froze. His head was still down, his eyes still closed.

I started forward, step by step. He was no more than a dozen steps away. Should I move slowly or rush it, counting on him having to wake up before he could react? I knew that both or neither might work—it was time to do what came naturally.

I charged into him, extending my arms like I was knocking a lineman out of the way, and shoved him and his chair. He flew through the air and toward the wall, slamming into it. He crashed down to the floor, and I grabbed the pistol. He yelled and tried to scramble to his feet.

I pointed the gun right at him. "Don't move a muscle or I'll shoot," I said. I suddenly realized I didn't know anything at all about guns—if there was a safety, if it was off, how to make it go off… I just had to hope he didn't realize I had no idea what I was doing.

He looked shocked and confused. Slowly he pulled himself into a sitting position. Then I noticed the dent in the wall, and the blood dripping from the side of his head. His eyes were glazed and glassy. He looked like he'd been concussed.

Charlie was right by my side. "We have to get out."

"The door is that way. You leave."

"What about you?"

"I have to stand guard so you can get away. Besides, I can't just leave Sir March here as their prisoner."

"We can go and get help."

"They could be gone before we get back. And what would I say to the police? That I'd helped some Russian spies kidnap the former head of British Security?"

"Not you. *We*," she said. "So what should *we* do?"

"Again, *we* shouldn't do anything. You leave and I'll think of something."

"What if we tied him up?"

"That could work if we had some rope or—" I looked at him. He had slid lower to the floor, his body at an awkward angle and his eyes closed.

"Is he dead?" Charlie asked.

"I didn't hit him that hard. Here, hold the gun." Gingerly, I handed her the pistol and went to his side. I gave him a little shove with my foot. Nothing. It was like pushing dead weight—hopefully, not *dead* dead weight. I reached down and placed my hand against his neck. I found a pulse—his heart was beating and he was breathing. He was unconscious though.

"He's alive, just unconscious. I hit him and then he hit his head. It's like a boxer knocking out his opponent."

I'd seen this happen on a football field but had never actually caused it.

"Maybe he's just pretending," Charlie said.

"Then he's a really good actor. But either way, I'll take care of it."

I undid his belt and pulled it free of the loops. Then I ripped open his shirt, the buttons flying off, and flipped him onto his stomach with his hands behind his back. There was no resistance or reaction. I pulled his shirt almost off and used the material to tie his hands together. I then took his belt and looped it around his hands, snugging it into place and tying it off.

"That should slow him down for a while."

"What now?" Charlie asked.

"Let me have the gun back."

"Gladly." She handed it to me.

"I'm going to go after Sir March," I said.

"Do you think that's wise?"

"I have a gun," I said.

"Do you know anything about firearms?"

"I've never even held a gun before," I said, "but I have played a lot of *Assassin's Creed*."

"Lovely. If we need a high score, you're the man to call," she said.

That was neither a kind nor an untruthful thing to say. What was I doing, suggesting that I was going to go after armed Russian spies, even if I was holding a gun? I would have the advantage only if we were having a showdown with PlayStation controllers. It didn't matter. I was doing it anyway.

"You don't have to come…you *shouldn't* come… I want you to be safe, but I can't just walk away," I said.

"I'm talking about *running* away," she said.

"I can't do that either. I'm going to try and get Sir March."

"Then I'm going too."

"I really don't think you should."

"And I don't think you should either, so we're doing this together," she said.

I took one more look at our prisoner. He was still unconscious and tied up like a calf at a rodeo.

Slowly, I pushed open the door leading into the other part of the building. Of course, Sir March might not still be here. Jack could have taken him away. But wouldn't I have noticed that on the monitors? Assuming, of course, that I had been awake when they left.

The warehouse was still dark, despite the rising sun. There were only a few windows in the building, and the ones that weren't smashed were covered by plywood. Charlie was tucked in so close behind me that when I stopped, she bumped into me.

"Sorry," she whispered.

I moved again, leading with the pistol. I didn't know if I could use it as a weapon, but it felt like a shield.

The building was huge and seemingly deserted. Jack must have taken Sir March away. If that was the case, there was nothing we could do but run. And then I heard voices. I tried to figure out where they were coming from. Charlie had heard them too and pointed off to the left. I nodded. Slowly, we started in that direction. The darkness and abandoned equipment helped hide us—and anything else out there.

As we crept closer, the voices got louder. It sounded like two voices, with different accents. I didn't know what I'd been expecting—maybe raised voices and cries of pain—but this sounded like a regular conversation.

I stopped and whispered to Charlie, "Stay here. If there's a problem, just stay put and hide. If they capture me, I'll tell them you already took off to get the police."

She nodded.

I circled around to the side instead of heading directly for the voices. I didn't want to lead them back to Charlie. Up ahead there was a patch of light, and I could see them, sitting in two chairs, facing each other. It did look like they were chatting, two friends having a friendly discussion. And, sure enough, one was Sir March. That made no sense...unless he was part of this, if his kidnapping had just been a ploy to get him away because he was really a Russian sleeper agent himself. Was he the Cambridge sixth? And then I noticed that he wasn't simply sitting in the chair—his hands were tied to the arms. There were marks on his face as if he'd been struck repeatedly. He was talking, but he wasn't a willing part of the discussion.

I moved from one piece of machinery to another, hidden in the darkness, until I was right behind Jack.

"You can be as stubborn as you wish," Jack was saying, "but sooner or later you will give me everything. Do not make this any harder on yourself."

"If I tell you the rest, will you let the young couple leave?" he asked.

"If I think you have told me everything, yes."

"I have told you a great deal about our plans to invade Europe," he said.

"Again with the Europe. I do not want to hear anything else about D-day or the Nazis. I want to know what you know about the sleeper cells," Jack said. He seemed frustrated, and he buried his head in his hands. This was my chance.

I came out of the shadows directly behind him.

"I am so tired," Jack said. "You must be tired too. Just tell me what I want to know."

Sir March was right in front of me. He saw me, and a small smile came to his face. I came closer and closer. I turned the gun around. I didn't know how to fire it, but I certainly could use it as a club. I jumped forward and brought the handle down on the side of Jack's head with a loud, sickening crack. He collapsed and fell to the floor.

"Bravo, David, bravo!" Sir March yelled.

I started toward Sir March, and he yelled, "Get his gun! Get his weapon!"

I turned, bent down and fumbled around the crumpled figure. He was wearing a holster under his jacket, and I removed the pistol from it. I now had two guns that I didn't know how to use. Charlie appeared out of the darkness and ran to Sir March. She started to pull at the ropes to release him.

I put one of the guns down on the floor and went to place a hand against Jack's neck to feel for a pulse. He reached out and grabbed for the gun, which was inches away from his fingertips. I kicked it away and then jumped back, holding my gun out in front of me. He tried to push himself up but fell back, landing on his butt.

"Don't move," I said.

He snarled at me. "You should put that gun down before you shoot yourself."

"It's not aimed at *me*."

"Stupid boy…are you going to shoot me?"

"If I need to…I will."

"I do not think you wish to shoot," he said. He got to his feet, and I took a small step backward. I had the gun, but I was the one who felt threatened and scared.

Then I had an idea. "Funny, your friend said the same thing—that I wouldn't shoot—but he looked pretty surprised when I shot him."

"If you shot Yuri, I would have heard it."

I had to think fast. What did they do in murder mysteries to muffle the sound? "A pillow makes a great silencer," I said. His expression changed to doubt. Maybe I'd convinced him. "It would be better to take you prisoner, but really, I don't care either way." I tried to sound confident and wished my voice hadn't cracked on the last few words.

Jack stopped moving forward and raised his hands.

"Get into that chair, and do it quickly before I change my mind about shooting you," I snapped.

Jack sat.

"Tie him up while I cover him," I said to Charlie.

Charlie picked up the pieces of rope that had been used on Sir March and tied them around Jack's wrists and ankles. Sir March checked each knot. Then he reached into his pocket and pulled out the keys to the cab.

"Our getaway vehicle," he said. "You don't mind us borrowing your cab, do you, Jack?"

Before Jack could answer, Sir March pushed the chair, and Jack tumbled over backward, crashing onto the floor.

"I didn't think he'd object." Sir March tossed me the keys.

Since the exit and the cab were both back toward the room where we'd been held, we went back in the direction we'd come. Charlie took Sir March by the arm, offering him assistance, hurrying him along.

"It's not far, Mr. March," I said.

"Mr. March? David, when did you stop calling me Bunny?"

"Sorry, Bunny, the exit is right ahead."

"Wait, we need to get our cell phones and your wallets and my bag," Charlie said.

"And we can check on the other guy," I said.

"I thought you shot him," Sir March—Bunny— said.

"Just a bluff. He's tied up too."

"Jolly good play, old man. First-rate!"

I pushed open the door. The man was on his feet, standing by the control panel that showed all the closed-circuit monitors, his hands still tied behind his back. I rushed over and swept his feet out from under him, and he crashed to the floor with a loud thud.

"Stay down," I ordered. I pushed him away from the control panel, and he sort of rolled across the floor. I had to admit, I was glad to see that he was alive and even happier to see that he was still tied up. This would hold him until long after we'd gotten away.

I grabbed the phones and my wallet and handed Charlie's bag to her.

"Look!" Charlie exclaimed. "There are people out there...people with guns!"

On one of the monitors we could see two men, dressed completely in black and carrying rifles. Another man appeared on a different monitor.

"Who are they?" Charlie exclaimed.

"They could be British security here to rescue us," I said.

"Or Russian agents. He might have hit a panic button and called for backup," Sir March said.

"What do we do?" Charlie asked.

I looked from one monitor to another. There was still nobody visible near the cab. They were coming in the other end of the building, and it was a big building. "We run."

We rushed out of the room. The door to the outside was right in front of us. I eased it open, and light streamed in. I peeked out. I couldn't see anybody. I motioned for Charlie and Sir March to follow. We climbed into the cab—me behind the wheel—and quietly closed the doors. I turned the key and the engine started with a roar. I had to back it up to get out. I started to inch along the narrow passage and then a man popped out of the door and ran toward us, weapon in hand!

"Hold on!" I screamed. I floored it, and the car careened down the alley, scraping and bouncing against the walls, sparks flying as metal hit brick. We popped out of the alley and I spun the wheel and slammed on the brakes, spinning us around. I hit the gas again and laid a patch of rubber as we squealed away.

I looked into the rearview mirror and the man, now joined by a second, was running down the alley, getting smaller and smaller as we sped away.

FIFTEEN

I pulled the cab onto a side street just down from the Underground station. I tried to climb out, but the door wouldn't open—it was jammed. I put my shoulder into it, and it finally popped out. No wonder we'd been attracting so many curious stares: the car was bashed and scraped, and a piece of metal was hanging down from the rear door.

I hauled open the back door, and it let out a loud groan. Charlie helped Sir March out of the cab. He seemed a little shaky on his feet, but after what he'd gone through, it was remarkable that he was even standing. Throughout the drive, he had kept muttering about the Nazis and how Churchill would be contacting Stalin to express his disapproval of the actions of their so-called allies. I knew Charlie thought I might be able to get information from him about my grandfather, but how could I believe any information he gave me? How could I trust somebody who seemed to have forgotten so many decades of his life?

"Where to?" Charlie asked.

"I'm not sure where *to*, but I'm sure where *from*. Let's get as far away from this cab as fast as we can."

"Leave the keys with the cab," Charlie said.

"Why would I do that?"

"Maybe somebody will steal it, and then they won't be able to trace our movements."

I tossed the keys in through the open window, and we headed down the stairs to the Tube. Charlie held on to Sir March on one side and I stayed on the other, not wanting to insult him but ready to grab him if he started to tumble.

"At least we'll be safe down here," Sir March said. "Even the German bombs can't reach this deep."

"You're right, we're safe," Charlie said. She looked at me and whispered, "Just go with it. There's nothing to be gained by arguing."

Charlie purchased tickets and we went down another level to the platform. All the way down, I kept looking over my shoulder to see if we were being followed. We were—by about a hundred people—but none of them looked suspicious. Then again, neither had Jack the cab driver or the couple by the Thames. It made me wonder about the overly friendly Canuck who'd bothered me in the lineup for the Eye.

Almost immediately, a train came whooshing into the station. We boarded and helped Sir March into a seat, then stood over him.

"So where should we go now?" I asked.

"Someplace out of the public eye. Someplace private," Charlie suggested.

"So we don't risk running into any more Russian spies or somebody looking for our little Bunny here," I said.

I looked down at Sir Bunny. His eyes were closed, his head angled off to the side; a little bit of drool was running out of the corner of his mouth. He was asleep.

"I guess we should try to get him back home," I said.

"And get ourselves arrested?" Charlie asked.

"We've got to do something. It's not like we can just leave him on the train."

"Maybe we could sort of drop him off at the door of a police station," Charlie suggested.

"That could work."

"Wait, I have an even better idea. We have to get off right here," she said.

The train was coming into a station. I roused Sir March. "Bunny, we have to get up." His eyes popped open, and I helped him stand up, both of us swaying as the train came to a stop. We helped him out onto the platform.

"I'm very tired," he said. "I really need to sit down...or have a nap."

"Exactly what I have in mind," Charlie said.

We took the escalator up to the surface.

"See that hotel?" Charlie said. "It's the perfect place to get out of the way of prying eyes and let Sir Bunny have a rest."

"That makes sense."

"I want you to go in and book a room. Pay them in cash, and we'll meet by the elevator."

The three of us entered the hotel lobby, and while Charlie and Sir March went off in one direction,

I headed for the front desk. It was a very swanky lobby, with a high ceiling and a big crystal chandelier hanging over an equally big fountain. Off to the side was a lounge area where lots of people were sitting, having drinks, talking, laughing—probably getting ready for New Year's Eve celebrations.

I walked up to the front desk and stood in front of a clerk. He looked up at me but didn't appear very interested.

When he finally spoke, all he said was, "Yes?"

"I'd like a room."

"I'm afraid since it's New Year's Eve, we are fully booked for the night."

"I don't want it for the night. Just for a few hours...until maybe seven or eight."

"Oh, I see," he said and gave me a wink. "I *understand.* Well, some of the rooms will not be needed until later this evening, and we do pride ourselves on being discreet."

I was pretty sure he didn't understand that I wanted the room so an old man we'd kidnapped could have a nap and we could hide out from Russian spies, British security and paparazzi.

"I am assuming you will be paying in cash," he said.

"Yes, cash."

"I just need you to fill in this registration information," he said as he pushed the form toward me.

This was a problem. A big problem. "Could you do without the form if I paid you double the price for the room and also provided a generous tip for a person at the front desk?"

He pulled the form away. "Perhaps we can do all of this, shall we say, off the record. The customer is always right." He took my money and slid a key card to me.

I went toward the bank of elevators. Charlie and Sir March were nowhere to be seen, and I wondered with horror if they'd been taken again. Then the door to one of the elevators popped open and Charlie stepped out and waved me over. I jumped in and pushed the button for the fourth floor. The door closed and we started up.

"Is this where the safe house is, David?" Sir March asked.

"Safe house...yes it is, Bunny." I knew from reading spy novels that a safe house was a place you went to hide when things had broken down. Things had definitely broken down for us.

The door opened on the fourth floor. I stepped out, looked both ways and gestured for them to follow. When we got into the room, I closed the door behind us and put on the deadbolt and the chain. I felt a rush of relief. We were safe.

"I'm so sorry to have put you to all this bother, especially after all you've already done for the service," Sir March said.

"That's all right," Charlie said. She gave me a knowing look. "You know David is always willing to do what SIS wants him to do. In fact, David was asking me for some clarification on his role...weren't you, David?"

"Yes, I was, if you could."

"I'm going around official channels, but I can do that. I owe you that after rescuing me twice in the last twenty-four hours. What would you like clarification on?"

What should I ask? If the first question was wrong, I might not get any answers at all. But if it all revolved around Kim Philby, the ringleader, that was where I had to start.

"How much can I trust Stanley?" I asked, using Philby's cryptonym.

"I think that's a question we've all asked ourselves," he said.

"And?"

"I believe you can trust him to continue to do what he is doing. He remains faithful to the cause."

"What cause?"

He gave me a strange look. "I'm not sure what you're asking, David."

I shook my head. "I'm not so sure myself. It's hard to know who's on what side."

"There's little doubt about Philby's allegiance—or yours and mine, for that matter."

Philby was a spy, a traitor, a sleeper, so his allegiance was clear. What was my grandfather's allegiance? Or Sir March's? Was it possible that the former head of SIS was actually working for the Russians? Was he the Cambridge sixth?

"Did you attend Cambridge?" I asked.

"You know full well that I went to Oxford—as did you."

"He knew that," Charlie jumped in. "He's just testing you."

"You'll have to come up with a better test than that...but I think I need to lie down first. I'm feeling a bit light-headed."

His legs buckled, and we grabbed him before he could collapse. I helped him onto one of the beds. He looked pale and tired and very old. This had been hard on all of us, but especially him. He needed to rest.

"Bunny, you go to sleep. I'll stand first watch," I said.

"Thank you, old friend. Make sure you wake me for my watch."

"Will do. Go to sleep."

"After he rests, you might get more information," Charlie said to me quietly.

"You might want to get some sleep as well. You have a big night ahead, and I wouldn't want you to fall asleep at eleven fifty-nine."

"Oh, my goodness," she said. "I need to answer some calls. Excuse me for a minute, please."

She got up and stepped into the hall, leaving the door slightly ajar. I went over to the door to flick off the light, throwing the room into darkness so Bunny could sleep. I should have stepped away. Instead, I took shelter behind the door. Curiosity was stronger than consideration or courtesy.

"Yes, I'm fine. I'm so sorry I didn't respond earlier...yes, it was inconsiderate...again, I'm sorry... well, it's hard to explain," Charlie said.

Hard to explain? Maybe if I could hear someone else explain this, I'd know what to say when it was my turn.

"Well, yes, he is with me...I'm downtown...close to where we're going to meet. We are still going to meet, aren't we?" she asked.

I waited for the answer. I knew what I wanted to hear.

"Good, good," she said. "I'll be there a little bit before midnight."

Not the answer I wanted. I guess he'd decided she was up to his standards.

"He's just a friend of the family," she said.

My ears perked up again. I was now part of this discussion, even though I wasn't on the phone.

"Well, yes, he *is* rather handsome, and he's a rugby player...if you have so many questions about him, perhaps you'd like me to bring him along and you could ask him yourself...fine..."

My phone buzzed, letting me know I'd received a text. I moved away from the door. Bunny was snoring. Good for him. I stepped into the bathroom, closed the door and pulled out my phone. As expected, it was from Steve.

Hey bro. News. Grandpa's journal has entry that he spoke to reporter in a little place just outside of Barcelona. Did some research–Philby filed a story dateline 2 days later from Barcelona. Doesn't mean they met but were in roughly the same place at the same time. What does this mean?

I texted back, I wish I knew.

SIXTEEN

There was a knock on the door, and I practically jumped out of my chair. I hadn't meant to fall asleep, but I had. There was more knocking, this time even louder. I moved through the darkness to the door.

"Hello?" I called out.

"Hello, it's Mr. Austin...from the front desk."

I looked through the peephole to make sure it was the clerk from the front desk. I opened the door.

"I need the room now, sir."

I looked at my watch. It was almost eleven o'clock!

"I'm so sorry. I fell asleep. We'll be right out."

"Quickly, please, sir. The maid will be here soon to make up the room for the regular guests."

I flicked on the light, and Charlie jumped to her feet.

"We have to get going! We fell asleep!" I said.

She looked at her watch. "The time! I have to get ready!" Charlie grabbed her bag and ran into the bathroom.

Sir March was still sound asleep. His eyes were closed, and he wasn't moving—he *was* breathing, wasn't he? He suddenly let out a loud, rasping snore. It was like music to my ears.

"Bunny, it's time to go. We have to leave," I said.

"Have we been discovered?"

"Yes, we have to leave."

He got up quickly. I knocked on the bathroom door. "We have to go."

"I'm almost ready."

"Do we have an escape route?" Sir March asked. "Should we go down the stairs or jump from rooftop to rooftop?"

"I was thinking the elevator."

"Excellent! Do the thing they'd least expect! You were always able to think through a strategy."

"Always?"

"Always."

I wanted to ask for more details, but this wasn't the time. Maybe in the cab I could ask him questions. I'd already decided I was going to get him back home as soon as possible.

Charlie came out of the washroom. She had changed into a short red dress and leggings that she must have had in her big purse, and she'd retouched her makeup and put up her hair. My mouth dropped open.

"So?" she asked.

"You do clean up good."

"I meant, what are we going to do now?" she said.

"First step is getting out of here."

She took Sir March by the arm, and we left the room and headed for the elevator.

"And then?"

"We'll get a cab. I'll drop you off by Trafalgar Square and then I'm going to take him home."

"You could get out with me and give the cabbie the address and fare and send him on his own the rest of the way," she suggested.

"I can't do that. I have to make sure he gets there safe and sound. There are Russian agents out looking for him."

"And looking for you. Besides, if you return home with him, you'll get caught by British security," she said.

"I'm going to drop him off at his front gate and then run like crazy."

I felt a heightened sense of anxiety as we exited the elevator and started through the lobby. The desk clerk caught my eye, saw Charlie and gave me a thumbs-up. Then he saw Sir March and looked confused—really confused.

I could see through the front windows that there was a line of cabs sitting right outside the front door. We would grab one—first making sure there wasn't a familiar Russian agent as the driver—and get on our way.

"Hey, if it isn't my good friend Nigel Finch!" a man called out. The man from the London Eye. He grabbed my hand and started shaking it. "Are you going to introduce me to your friends?"

"We're really in a hurry." He still had my hand in his, and he tightened his grip.

"I think we should sit down for a drink, although really, there's no need for introductions. I know of both Sir March and Charlie...although I do prefer the name Charlotte so much more."

How could he possibly know their names? Unless...

He raised his left hand. There was a newspaper draped over it, and underneath, barely visible, was a pistol. "Let's just sit down and talk. Talking is a much better alternative."

He finally released my hand and gestured toward the lounge. We found an open table, and he motioned for us to sit. Charlie and I flanked him, and Sir March sat across from him. He put the newspaper and hidden gun on the table beside his right hand.

"As you must now know, I'm not a friendly Canadian tourist."

"I didn't think you were Canadian to begin with. How did you find us?"

"That reminds me. Could I have my pen back?"

"Your pen? Wait..." I pulled it out of my pocket. "This is yours?"

"I slipped it into your pocket when I was having that picture taken. It has a tracking device inside."

He took the pen from me and examined it. "I'm glad it's fine. Do you have any idea how expensive these are?"

"Glad I kept it safe for you. But why did you want to follow me to begin with?" I asked.

"The same reason the Russians were after you and the SIS was chasing you. Then, of course, there were the paparazzi and those private detectives."

"Private detectives?" I asked.

"Yes, apparently they were hired to investigate you," he said, pointing to Charlie.

"Why would anybody investigate me?" she demanded.

"You can expect your privacy to be invaded when you date a member of the royal family."

"You're dating royalty?" I gasped.

"There are lots of royals in England. It's not like he's next in line to the throne."

"Close enough," the man said.

Great! I'd been in competition with a prince or an earl or a duke or something. I'd never had a chance—not that I'd ever really have a chance with somebody as incredible as Charlie. Well, at least I wasn't losing out to some common git.

"Who are you?" I asked.

"That's not your concern."

"CIA," Sir March said. "I recognize the clothing, the expensive tracking device in the pen and, of course, that smug smell of superiority."

"You're CIA?" I said to the man. "But we're on the same side!"

"Everybody is on their own side," Sir March said.

"Or a few sides," the man added.

"What do you want with us?" I asked.

"I want you two to walk away," he said, pointing first at me and then at Charlie.

"We can just leave?" Charlie asked.

"Walk away and nobody will know you're involved. Go—enjoy your New Year's celebration. If you leave right now, you won't even be late."

"What about Sir March?" I asked.

"Believe me, we'll take good care of him."

"You'll return him to his home?" I asked.

"Eventually."

"What does that mean?"

"We have a few questions we'd like to ask him," he said.

"Like the Russians do."

"Perhaps the same questions but using different methods. You two should run along now."

Charlie went to stand up, but I said, "We're not going anywhere without him. He comes with us." Charlie looked confused and upset, but she sat back down.

"Do you really think you're in a position to make demands?" he asked. "Not only do I have the weapon, but I also have the two young people who kidnapped Sir Bunny March. Even if I don't shoot you, do you know how much trouble you'll be in when I turn you in to the authorities?"

"Less trouble than you," Sir March said. I wasn't aware that he'd even been paying attention to what was going on. "You should look under the table."

"What?" the man asked.

"Look under the table...all of you."

I looked. Sir March was holding a pistol, and it was aimed right at the CIA agent's crotch!

"I think you should slowly move your right hand away from the newspaper," Sir March said.

The agent looked down at the paper, but his hand remained in place. I thought about reaching for it, but I wasn't sure I could beat him to it.

"I am very old, but I can still pull the trigger faster than you can reach that gun."

"Do you really think you can get away with shooting me in the lounge of a hotel, in front of dozens of people?" he asked.

"I don't expect to get away with it. I shoot you and the police will come, and I will be arrested...and then released. I am a member of the Empire, a knight, a former head of SIS."

"That won't be enough to let you get away with it."

"Perhaps not, but I'm also an old man whose mind goes in and out. What are they going to do to me, take away my tapioca pudding?" He laughed.

"My government won't let you get away with this," he said.

"Your government will disavow any knowledge of you. Don't you think they're just going to look for any excuse to distance themselves from claims that they authorized you to kidnap and interrogate me? I'd be surprised if they even admit they know who you are. Now, move your hand."

The man slowly withdrew his hand. Without thinking, I reached forward and took the newspaper and gun.

"Good work, David."

Charlie and I started to get up, and this time Sir March motioned for us to stay. We slumped back into our seats.

"First, give me the keys to your vehicle," Sir March said to the man.

"I don't have any—"

"You really want to get shot, don't you? Is your Mercedes really worth a gunshot wound?"

"Is it a white Mercedes?" I asked.

"Probably. The Russians like black BMWs, and the CIA drive white Mercedes. They might as well put a sign on the door that says *spies inside.* Give me the keys."

The man pulled the keys out of his pocket.

"David," Sir March said. I took the keys.

"Try to drive a little more carefully than you did with the cab," the man said.

"Where is it?" Sir March asked.

"Right out front. You can't miss it."

"Now I want you to speak into your little microphone and tell your two colleagues to get up and leave the lounge," Sir March said.

"What are you talking about?" the man asked.

"One is sitting at the bar, pretending to read a magazine, and the second is at the table right by the entrance. I'm sure they can both hear me. They need to leave right now. Tell them to leave."

"Both of you leave the building," the agent said into his lapel.

"No, I do not want them to leave the building. I want them to walk right over to the fountain in the lobby and take a seat...*in* the fountain."

"What?"

"In the fountain."

"You're joking."

"No joke. I want to make sure that every single person in this hotel sees them and makes note of them, so that if we're followed, it will also be noticed." Sir March leaned forward and spoke louder. "I know you can both hear me. Do as I've suggested or I shoot your agent."

I watched as the two men got up and slowly started to walk out. One of them gave us a long, hard look as he went toward the exit, where the second man was already waiting. We watched as they walked over to the fountain, stepped over the retaining wall and sat down in the water. The whole lobby noticed.

People laughed and stared and pointed, and a hotel employee came over and started yelling at them.

"Now it's your turn," Sir March said.

"I'd rather be shot than sit in the fountain."

"No fountain. I want you to go into the washroom—the women's washroom. Now get going."

The CIA agent got to his feet. If looks could kill, we'd all be dead right there at the table.

"You go in there and stay in there. If I see you peeking out, I'm going to shoot off whatever is sticking out."

"I'm not going to forget this," the agent said.

"And I probably will...maybe before the day is over. Go."

As the agent started to walk away, we all got up. Charlie offered Sir March a hand.

"Take the newspaper and gun. We'll leave it in the car when we abandon it," he said. The agent disappeared into the washroom. "Let's go."

We hurried as fast as Sir March's legs would carry him. Out of the lounge, past the fountain and its two bathers—who had now drawn a large crowd—and out through the revolving door.

"There it is!" Charlie exclaimed.

It was a big white Mercedes—the one that had followed us before. I hit a button on the key fob, the car's lights flashed, and we jumped in. I started it up, threw it into Drive and took off. Pulling out, I clipped the fender of the car in front of me. So much for being careful. We raced off.

SEVENTEEN

We drove a few blocks and then abandoned the Mercedes, bashed-in fender and all. As I pulled over, I deliberately brushed a telephone pole to give the other fender a matching look. Sir March said he was certain the car had a tracking device as well, so we had to get far away from it before the agents' backup could locate us. We jumped into a cab and headed for Trafalgar Square.

Sir March had gone back to staring into space and muttering things about the Nazis.

"I don't get it," I whispered to Charlie. "One minute he's like James Bond, and the next he's, well, like this."

"My grandmother was like that too. Some things she could do well, like nothing was wrong. Mainly things from when she was a lot younger."

"So he became a spy again."

"Exactly."

I guessed that made sense.

"Now if only the taxi could go faster," Charlie said.

We were barely moving, jammed in bumper-to-bumper traffic. I kept looking through the back window for black BMWs, white Mercedes, motorcycles or cabs—which made up pretty much half the vehicles on the road.

"Can't you go any faster?" Charlie asked the driver.

"Not unless I go up on the sidewalk, and I don't think I'd make much progress there either."

He was right. It wasn't only the road that was blocked; the sidewalks were packed with people walking, singing and drinking. Almost everybody was moving in the same direction as us—toward Trafalgar Square.

"How much farther is it?" I asked.

"A dozen or so blocks," Charlie answered.

"It's eleven forty-five. I know this is important, but I don't think we'll get there in time. I'm sorry," I said.

"I could walk faster than this!"

"And if you did walk, could you get there by midnight?" I asked.

"I could, but there's no way Sir Bunny could walk that far or that fast," she said.

"He doesn't have a date, and neither do I. I'm taking him home, remember? Go, get out, walk."

"I can't just leave you two here," she protested.

"We'll be fine. Get out and get going before it's too late. You'll miss your...appointment." Somehow I couldn't bring myself to say the word *date.*

She hesitated. I knew she wanted to go but also felt bad about leaving us.

"Don't worry. I'll get him home. I'm just sorry I can't spend New Year's with my favorite lady, but I hope your nana will understand that I wanted to be with her."

She laughed. "I'm getting out. Stop the cab," she said to the driver.

Since we were barely moving, that was an easy request. She opened the door and jumped out.

"Be safe...I'll call you tomorrow...I'll be over tomorrow...I promise," she said.

"Sure, see you tomorrow. Now go, or you'll miss him!"

She gave us one more smile and then raced away, getting quickly swallowed up by the crowd as a wave of sadness washed over me. Some part of me had hoped—believed—that maybe she wouldn't go, that she would stay with me. I should have known better. She was going to meet a prince, not be with a pauper.

"Driver, you can turn around. We're not going to Trafalgar Square anymore. Take me to Coventry Lane, please."

"Sure thing."

"No, wait," Sir March said. "You don't have to go all that way. I can get there by myself."

"I have to make sure you get there safely."

"I think between myself and the driver, I'll be fine."

Part of me wanted to agree and get out of the cab, maybe even run after Charlie, but I couldn't leave him alone. He needed my help.

"Sorry, sir. I can't do that."

"Yes, you can. DJ, you need to go after your girl."

"She's not my girl and—what did you call me?"

"DJ, which is short for David Junior, named after David McLean Senior, your grandfather."

I was shocked. I stared at him and saw something different. He looked *all there.*

"I know you're surprised, and perhaps I shouldn't be telling you any of this, but after all you've been through, I feel you deserve to know the truth," he said.

His voice was steady, his words clear and concise, his eyes bright.

"I am Bernard March. I am the former head of MI6. I am also very much in possession of my faculties."

"But...but how...why...?"

"Let me try to explain. As you are aware, your passport sounded an alarm when you entered the country. In the process of clearing you, the large amount of cash and the false passports in your pack were discovered."

"But they didn't find them in my bag. They stopped searching before they found them."

"They were stopped before they found them the *second* time. They wanted you to be unaware they had found them. The discovery of the false passports, particularly one with the name Nigel Finch, triggered even more alarms—alarms that pulled me out of my long retirement."

"But how does that involve the Russians and Americans?"

"Your quest for answers alerted them both, and that's when we saw an opportunity. In taking me away, you allowed the Russians to gain access to all the information floating around in the head of a former director, information they could extract from me in my, shall we say, reduced capacity."

"But why would you want to give them information?"

"There is information and then there is false information. Right now, the two Russian agents have hightailed it to their embassy, where they are reporting this significant intelligence coup."

"This was all a trick?"

"Counterintelligence is done with smoke and mirrors."

"But they could have killed us; they beat you up."

"I've had worse beatings from better interrogators. Besides, we were covered. There were agents and surveillance outside the building at all times. Those men we saw on the monitors were British SIS getting ready to break into the building."

"Then why didn't they just come in and...Wait! the Russians had to get away. How did you know we'd be able to escape?"

"I didn't. We had another plan in place—not nearly as dangerous as the one you executed," he explained.

"I guess I'm sorry."

"Nothing to be sorry about."

"I understand about the Russians, but why would the CIA try to interrogate you? Aren't they on our side?"

"As I said before, everybody is on their own side." He smiled. "Although, believe me, the CIA is going to be paying for that little error in judgment. You know, your grandfather would have been proud of the way you handled yourself."

"You did know him, right?"

"Very well. Very well indeed."

"Then you need to tell me about him, about what he was, what he was doing. Was he a spy or a double agent? A sleeper or a traitor?"

"I've already told you much more than I should have."

"You have to tell me! You owe me that much."

"DJ, let's say I did tell you. I gave you answers. I told you all about him. Would you believe me?"

"Why wouldn't I believe you?"

"After all you've seen, all you've been through, do you still feel that you can believe anything? This whole world of espionage, intelligence and counter-intelligence is nothing more than a journey through the looking glass."

I thought about what he had said. How *could* I believe anything? I shook my head.

"Tell me about your grandfather," he said.

"What do you mean?"

"Tell me about your grandfather."

"He was my grandfather."

"But what sort of person was he?"

"I'm not so sure anymore."

"Yes, you are. Tell me about him, the things you know for *certain*."

I thought about it before I answered. "He loved to tell stories and jokes. He played golf. He liked everybody. He always said strangers were friends you hadn't met yet. He was always there for his daughters and grandchildren. He was kind and decent... and honest."

"He was also somebody I'd trust with my life. Somebody I *did* trust with my life. He was somebody who always did what needed to be done," Sir March said.

That's what it said in the notebook. *I always did what needed to be done. Nothing more and nothing less.*

"Isn't that enough for you to know?" he asked.

"I guess it is."

"Good. Now get out of the cab and go after that girl."

"I don't think she wants me to go after her."

"And I think you don't know what you're talking about. She was practically begging you to go after her." He extended his hand, and we shook. "It was a pleasure—but you know that none of this ever happened."

"None of what?"

He laughed.

"It is all right for me to leave you? What if there are other Russian agents around?"

"I think they'd be foolish when you consider that our cab driver is also one of our agents."

The driver turned around and gave a slight wave of his hand.

"And the cab in front of us contains two more MI6 agents. Not to mention the car three back, with three more agents. I think we'll be able to *just* get by without your assistance, although your not wanting to send me home alone...well, that shows real class. You weren't prepared to abandon the helpless old man even when it put you in danger. Now you know I'm safe, so you have to go...*now*!"

I jumped out of the cab and went to close the door, then stopped. I had one more question. "David McLean—that really was my grandfather's name, right?"

"His name...and yours. Goodbye, David McLean."

I closed the door and hurried off.

EIGHTEEN

I moved through the throng of people. They all were happy and laughing and enjoying the gigantic street party. I glanced at my watch. It was almost the New Year—time for a fresh start, a new beginning. The music got louder as I got closer to Trafalgar Square. I could see Nelson's Column in the distance, but I wasn't going to make it in time. The crowd had almost become a solid mass, and I could do no more than shuffle forward a few inches at a time. I wondered if Charlie had been able to push through to get to her date. I hoped she had...no, I hoped she got what she wanted. She deserved that.

A loud, metallic voice came from a PA system. It started to count down to the New Year. There was a huge explosion, and a roar went up from the crowd. The entire sky lit up as fireworks shot into the air. With each explosion, the crowd roared again, faces lit up. Car horns honked, noisemakers squawked and people jumped up and down, screaming. Couples hugged and kissed, and handshakes were offered all around. Glasses were raised in toasts, and people in the crowd were singing. And I was alone. I had no one to hug or even shake hands with—

"Happy New Year!" a girl yelled in my face. She grabbed me and gave me a big hug and a kiss.

"Happy New Year to you—"

She was already off, kissing the next person in the crowd. Here I was, alone in the middle of a gigantic crush of people. I shuffled sideways until I was shielded by a storefront and then pulled out my phone. I'd send a greeting to the only person I felt like sending a greeting to.

Happy New Year, bro. Hope you are bringing in the New Year in style with Laia. See you in a few days. Love, DJ

I stayed sheltered against the wall as the fireworks went on and on, bigger and brighter until there was a final explosion and the crowd went wild. Then the last burst fell from the sky and it was over. The crowd started clapping and cheering, and I joined in. It *had* been quite the show.

I edged forward. I wanted at least to be able to say that I'd been in Trafalgar Square at New Year's instead of close to it. That was part of it. The other part was that I wanted to make sure Charlie was okay, that she'd made it, that she was safe.

The fireworks had stopped, but the party was continuing. The music began playing again. It was practically wall-to-wall people, and everybody was friendly and happy. More than a few people had had a little liquid happiness poured into them. I really was at a gigantic party, yet I couldn't help but feel like the uninvited guest who didn't know anybody.

Nelson's Column soared up directly in front of me. I was close enough that I could see the giant lions guarding it. Off to both sides were big, beautiful, brightly lit fountains. People waded in both of them, celebrating and cheering. I couldn't help but think of the CIA agents in the fountain at the lobby.

That had been fun. Behind the fountains, in the distance, were the steps of the National Gallery. That's where she was meeting him.

It would be good—and awful—to see them together, but at least I'd know she was safe and that she'd gotten what she wanted. Maybe I could even go up and wish them both a Happy New Year—and give him a piece of my mind. Anybody who had to question whether she was up to his "standards" didn't deserve to be with her in the first place. I didn't care if he was royalty. I didn't care if he was the King of England. I'd just go up to him and—

"Hello."

"Charlie!" She was standing right in front of me. "Didn't you make it?"

"I made it," she said.

That could only mean one thing. He had decided not to show. "I'm so sorry that he wasn't there."

"He was there."

"But—but what happened?"

"Now you look as confused as he did," she said. "I told him I'd made a mistake. He wasn't the person I wanted to kiss at the stroke of midnight."

I didn't know what to say.

"And yes, I do mean you and not Sir Bunny. Where is he?"

"He's safe and on his way home...but...me...you want to be with me? Why?"

"Because you took my nana to the top of a mountain and took care of her. Because you wear your grandfather's beret. Because you saved my life. Because you couldn't abandon an old man in a warehouse. Because I hope that you think I'm up to your standards and, most of all, because you still blush a little whenever you look at me."

She got up on her tiptoes and wrapped her arms around my neck, and the world seemed to explode in flashes. We were surrounded by paparazzi, cameras out, flashes going off.

"I think they finally got that picture they wanted," I said.

"Not yet. Let's give them something worth taking a picture of."

She reached up even higher, and we kissed.

NINETEEN

JANUARY 3

I looked up at the big board announcing arrivals. My mother's flight had just landed in Toronto, and she and Aunt Debbie would be through customs soon. The plan had always been for me to pick them up after the cruise. What they wouldn't know was that *my* plane had gotten in from London an hour before their flight, and I'd just cleared customs and stashed my bag in the trunk of the car. I'd had time to send a couple of texts—one to Steve to tell him I had landed, and the other to Spencer, telling him I was back from my adventure and would be picking up his mother along with mine and driving her home. Neither had answered back yet.

Now that I was standing here in the airport, the whole last week seemed like a strange dream. Spies, guns, being kidnapped and held hostage, assorted car chases...somehow, those things all seemed more real than my time with Charlie. We'd spent the entire time on the first and second of January pushing Doris around London in a wheelchair, seeing the sights and meeting what seemed like all of her wonderful family, who were so kind to me. Except for Charles, who was still a git.

It was all pretty unbelievable. And, of course, unworkable. We lived six time zones and one big ocean apart. She was moving on with her life, and I was going on with mine. Still, we'd agreed that I'd come back—as originally planned—for a couple of weeks during the summer, along with my brother, Steve. I had to admit, I understood better now why he'd had to get back to Spain so soon.

I was looking forward to seeing my mother. I figured I'd let her settle in for a few days before I told her where I'd been and what I'd discovered. Before any of the cousins did anything, though, we all had to talk—share what we'd discovered and agree on what we were going to tell our parents. That meeting, I was looking forward to. What came after we told our parents, not so much.

The big doors slid open and my mother appeared, pulling her suitcase, pushed along with the crowd of other passengers. She waved and smiled when she saw me, and I waved back. I was so happy to see her. But where was Auntie Debbie?

I ran over and threw my arms around her. It was good to have her back safe and sound.

"How was the trip?" I asked.

"Very relaxing, for the most part."

"Where's Auntie Debbie?"

"Unfortunately, she got called away on business and had to leave early. And how were things with you?"

Her tone of voice worried me. "Things were good, fine, uneventful."

"Really? If this is uneventful, I wonder what you'd consider an event."

She handed me a newspaper. It was opened to a photo of me and Charlie in Trafalgar Square, kissing. The headline said, *Our Charlie with a Colonial*!

My mouth dropped open. “I can explain.”

“I’m sure you can, and you will,” she said. “But before that, I have one question. Is she a nice girl?”

“Top two,” I replied.

“Who’s the other?”

I pointed at her, and she laughed. “If you think you’re going to charm your way out of this one, well, you’re probably right. And you’re going to have to tell me everything.”

“I can tell you,” I said. “Of course, that doesn’t mean you’re going to believe me. It all began at the cottage…”

ACKNOWLEDGMENTS

Throughout the book, I've embedded subtle and not-so-subtle references to some of the great mystery, spy and adventure novels I've read over the years. My thanks to all of those incredible writers who inspired and entertained me...see if you can find all the references.

Eric Walters began writing in 1993 as a way to entice his grade-five students into becoming more interested in reading and writing. At the end of the year, one student suggested that he try to have his story published. Since that first creation, Eric has published over eighty novels and picture books. Many of his works have become bestsellers, and he has won over one hundred awards. Often his stories incorporate themes that reflect his background in education and social work and his commitment to humanitarian and social-justice issues. He is a tireless presenter, speaking to over 70,000 students per year in schools across the country and throughout North America. Eric has three grown children and he lives in Mississauga, Ontario, with his wife and two dogs. To find out more about Eric, visit his website at www.ericwalters.net. *Sleeper* is the sequel to *Between Heaven and Earth*, Eric's novel in Seven (the series).

9781459805439 pb
9781459805446 pdf
9781459805453 epub

9781459805408 pb
9781459805415 pdf
9781459805422 epub

9781459805491 pb
9781459805507 pdf
9781459805514 epub

9781459805316 pb
9781459805323 pdf
9781459805330 epub

9781459805378 pb
9781459805385 pdf
9781459805392 epub

9781459805460 pb
9781459805477 pdf
9781459805484 epub

9781459805347 pb
9781459805354 pdf
9781459805361 epub

9781459808256 pb
9781459808270 epub
9781459808263 pdf

www.thesevensequels.com